Realm of
Angels

Book 1

Light

J. R. Thomas

Origins and Destinies Publications

Published by:

Origins and Destinies
Australia
Contact: www.jrthomas.com.au

Copies of this book may be ordered through booksellers or by contacting the publisher directly through the above website.

Because of the dynamic nature of the Internet, any web addresses or links contained in this book may have been changed since publication and may no longer be valid. The views expressed in this work are solely those of the author and do not necessarily reflect the views of the publisher, and the publisher hereby disclaims any responsibility for them.

Cover image © Thinkstock Images

ISBN: 978-0-9923014-2-2 (sc)

Realm of Angels Book 1 - Light
by J R Thomas 1968 -
Christian Fiction

Date: 13 Sept 2014

For my brother, Mark,
and my sisters, Andrea and Kym,
who shared my childhood days ...

- playing under the sprinkler
- dodging 'the pink stick', 'the pinchy-man',
  horse-bites, toe-twists, and Chinese burns
- body-surfing at King's Beach
- riding on Jean's back
- chasing the chooks
- throwing things off the lookout tower
- picnicking in the triangle
- riding down 'the hill' - no feet
- making 'dribbly sandcastles'
- eating broadbeans, chokos, goulash,
  Texan hash, perrys, and dippy-eggs

. . . and all that time
we were entertaining angels unawares!

Part One

Chapter One

Gilliad hovered, weightless, suspended on the timeless eve of eternity past.

It was hard to put into words what it felt like to suddenly exist. There was nothing he could compare with the awareness of being he felt at that moment. He was not, and then, in a breath, he was. Simple as that ... the beginning.

His head turned slowly as he took in his surroundings for the first time. There were echoes in the darkness beyond – remnants of the roar of a mighty rushing wind, but it had passed and the echoes were dissipating, growing fainter.

His eyes took in the great void of darkness behind, above, and below him: darkness that seemed to stretch on forever. But Gilliad knew that it was not to the darkness he belonged. The darkness did not call to him.

Vivid colours danced and swirled around him, bathing him in warmth. It was almost as if the colours could be felt, touched, absorbed: colours that came from the light.

The light shone dispelling the darkness. The light was pure. It beckoned and Gilliad obeyed its call, his heart pounding as he drew near. He was not afraid, but something within him sensed that the light was to be approached carefully and with great respect and reverence.

As he came closer to the light, Gilliad became aware of other beings around him, for from the far reaches of the darkness, thousands upon thousands of heavenly hosts were descending, drawn by the light. Beings strong and powerful, they moved towards the light as one, faces glowing, reflecting the light.

The air was charged with life and movement.

But Gilliad had only one thought ... the light. The light emitted a warmth which penetrated his very soul, and his inner being trembled with the awareness that the light knew all about him. The light had made him. The light loved him.

Gilliad belonged to the light. In the light there was life.

Gilliad's feet alighted, and looking down he found himself standing in what seemed to be a huge courtyard paved by an expanse of smooth stone which shimmered in front of him. He took a few tentative steps and then stopped. But the light continued to beckon; to draw him towards it.

He started forward again towards the light – one foot, the other foot – taking in every new sensation: the gentle breeze, the pure ethereal melody that surrounded him, the fresh scent of blossoms which delicately perfumed and seemed almost to be part of the air that formed his breath, and the feel of his sandalled feet on the hard, smooth stone.

He quickened his pace and began to ascend the paving, which now sloped steadily upwards. The courtyard had merged into a wide pathway leading to steps which were carved out of solid, glossy white stone, but Gilliad barely noticed as he placed one foot in front of the other. He was aware of fleeting glimpses of beauty as he passed: scenes he sensed that, if he took the time to pause and look, would take his breath away.

But the light drew him onward.

He entered a large building, but he looked neither up nor down, to the left nor to the right.

As he drew nearer, the presence of the light captivated him. The intense brilliance of ruby, gold, magenta, crimson, deep emerald, tangerine, and fuchsia that surrounded and came from within the light misted his vision as if he were walking through a fine spray of tiny droplets, and he blinked several times and slowed his approach.

The light began to take on form, and as he peered through the shroud of mist, the image of a throne, large and imposing, began to appear through his clouded vision.

Gilliad felt himself falling to his knees. His breath drew sharply into his lungs and he felt as if the entire meaning of his existence had, in that moment, that one brief moment, been revealed.

And it had. For Gilliad knew that the One who sat on the throne was the reason he existed.

As he knelt, Gilliad felt himself gently lifted to his feet by hands unseen, and a voice that seemed to come from beyond eternity – a voice of wisdom – of deep and ancient knowledge – spoke from the throne.

'I am the Father of your spirit. From My breath you were formed.'

Wave after wave of tremors began to rise from Gilliad's inner being and shake his body, and his knees threatened to buckle. A pounding which had begun in his ears threatened to drown out all other sound, and his breath came in sporadic gasps, rapid and shallow. But Gilliad held his gaze steady, his eyes unable and unwilling to focus on anything but the vision before him – the One on the throne – the One who had made him – who gave him life and who loved him.

And as he stood there transfixed, his feet one with the cool stone beneath him, he heard the voice of the Father say, 'This is My beloved Son. We are One.' And as Gilliad's gaze followed the outstretched hand of the Father, he found himself looking deep into the eyes of the Son, and there he found truth and love, kindness and mercy. And in that one moment, he knew that he would always, always, remember the eyes of the Son.

'I love you.' The gentle voice of the Father seemed to be speaking directly to Gilliad.

Love. Was that was he felt now? If this was love, he wanted for nothing more.

'I made you for a reason,' the Father continued. 'You have a purpose, a mission. It will soon be revealed.'

A reason. A purpose. A mission. 'I ...' was all Gilliad managed, for he had no words for how he felt.

But words were not needed.

Gilliad could no more contain in his heart the joy that surged from within him than contain forever the breath of air that had entered his lungs. He threw up his arms and burst into song, praise rising from his heart: a heart overflowing with the love that he felt for the Father and the Son; a heart overflowing with the joy of knowing their love given freely to him.

And the heavens were filled with the celestial harmony of thousands upon thousands of angelic voices extolling their Maker, celebrating the love of the Father for the Son, the Son for the Father, celebrating the joy of being loved. Of just being.

And the symphony of praise echoed into the great void of darkness, filling it with the sounds of life.

Gilliad looked around him, his eyes slowly taking in his surroundings. The Father's home was imposing, yet at the same time intimate – a sanctuary.

He was standing inside a spacious building crafted of white stone. He walked over to one of the walls and traced his finger along a joint. Each stone was set so that the joints between the stones were almost invisible. His eyes followed the wall to its top. The ceiling soared above his head, supported by wide round pillars.

He looked down at the surface beneath his feet. It was hard and smooth with no joints; at least none that he could see from where he stood. It seemed to be a huge expanse of polished stone of some sort. The floor was marbled and reflected the light, throwing off swirls of colour which seemed to bounce off the walls; even bounce off each other – tiny prisms of light; slivers of iridescence. Gilliad swiped at the air, closing his fist upon one. He opened it and looked, but the prism had vanished.

The Father's throne sat in the centre of an elevated platform at the edge of which burned fragrant incense in large golden bowls, and the smoke of the incense drifted in fine curling wisps, dancing with the tiny prisms of colour and perfuming the sanctuary. In front of the platform lay an altar: a simple slab of polished white stone.

To the right of the Father's throne was the throne of the Son; no less ornate and imposing. And the Spirit – the life of the Father – flowed through the Son, for Father, Son, and Spirit were One.

Winged angels – cherubim and seraphim – surrounded the throne singing praises, giving glory to their Maker. 'Holy, holy is the Lord of hosts,' they sang. Their harmony was effortless as if they *were* the music and they were only giving of themselves. Their gentle melody drifted, filled the temple, and was carried on the air beyond the walls.

Led by the Son, the angels left the sanctuary, descended the wide steps, and followed the paving until they came to a thick wall which lay along one side of the courtyard.

The wall was built of solid stone which, on close inspection Gilliad noticed, was flecked with reds, yellows, and browns. From a distance, however, these tiny glistening flecks of colour had given the wall a deep, rich coppery hue which made the wall shimmer as if alive. The foundations of the wall were studded with jewels of every kind which also seemed to come to life as the light hit each perfectly crafted surface, bouncing off tiny coloured prisms like the ones in the sanctuary.

The spacious courtyard was filled with the buzz of many voices, and Gilliad stood tall, craning his neck, his eyes focussed on the face of the Son. Slowly, a great gate in the wall opened, and after signalling the angels to gather around the opening, the Son turned and stood in the gap between heaven and the blackness beyond.

Gilliad found himself being swept along with the vast number of heavenly hosts who ascended to the top of the thick wall. Here some sat, others stood. Still others hovered in the heavens above the wall, watching, waiting.

Gilliad's vision began to adjust. He could see a large dark mass below: a great ball of matter suspended in the void of darkness.

The Son slowly raised His arms and as He did, the life and power of the Spirit proceeded from the Father through the Son and enveloped the mass below, hovering over the surface of the dark waters that covered the mass, bringing the mass to life.

Suddenly, a loud voice came from the throne, 'Let there be light.'

The contrast again assaulted Gilliad's eyes, but he could not look away. As he watched, the Father commanded the light to separate from the darkness and the mass began to move, tumbling slowly, rotating on its invisible axis deep within its core. Evening then morning.

And still the Son stood, His arms outstretched towards the earth.

When the tumbling mass had reached full revolution, the Father commanded the raging waters that covered the great mass to separate, and waters began to rise from the surface of the earth. From Gilliad's vantage point high in the heavens, it looked as if the mass below him had become enveloped by a fine mist, buffering it from the dark void – the endless infinity of space.

And still the mass turned steadily, powerfully. Evening then morning.

As the turbulent waters that covered the mass roared and tossed under the power of the Spirit of the Creator, He commanded them to part, and the earth heaved and groaned as it buckled under the force as the waters fled to their allotted courses, moulding mountains, valleys, and plains: vast expanses of land between the deep dark oceans and wild, restless seas.

As Gilliad watched, the same voice of authority that commanded the light to appear and the waters to part called, 'Come down here.'

All of a sudden, Gilliad found himself being pulled from the heavens. He plunged forward into the darkness, his arms pinned to his side, and he hurtled head first towards the spinning mass of land and seas. He managed to turn himself as he passed through the misty shroud below and he attempted to land on his feet but he misjudged the incline, rolling once, twice, before finding his footing.

When he reached out to steady himself, Gilliad started, for under his hand tiny blades of green had begun to spring up, quickly covering the red-brown soil. He ran his palm lightly over the surface and worked his fingertips into the coolness underneath where roots had begun their journey deep into the damp earth.

Gilliad lay down on the soft grass. He felt slightly dazed. His thoughts were racing: a jumbled mass of pictures, words, feelings that were new and strange. He was aware of others around him: some also lying, some sitting staring into the air, or examining the grass, the soil, examining themselves.

Gilliad lay like this for some time, and in the quietness, his mind began to drift as he stared into the sky. His eyes slowly glazed over.

Suddenly, the ground began to vibrate and Gilliad sat up. He tried to find his footing but quickly gave up. Balancing himself on one knee as best he could, he spread both hands out and tried to grip onto the short blades of grass but found himself being heaved off balance again. Finding nothing to grab onto, he went tumbling headlong into a tall grey pillar.

Whump. The pillar didn't budge. Nor was it, by any stretch of the imagination, soft like the grass.

'Humph,' he added to other 'humphs' that came from the vicinity of some of the other tall grey pillars.

Gilliad righted himself and looked around, rubbing his head and grunting, the breath quite knocked out of him. He leant up against the pillar, trying to regain his bearings.

The rumbling and heaving had quieted now and was replaced by a gentle, wind-like swishing – a rustling sort of sound. Where there had previously stood grassy hills and valleys, stark rocky outcrops, and muddy banks or wide bare stretches of sand leading down to the water, all manner of trees, ferns, bushes, and shrubs had now sprouted from the earth: deep green dense foliage, pale fine-leafed fragrant herbs, glossy wax-leafed plants, and fine fern fronds hiding under leafy canopies.

Gilliad stood leaning against the tree, his mouth gaping as he looked around him. Buds had begun to form on many of the plants and beautiful flowers quickly appeared as the buds began to unfurl: petals resplendent in shades of red, blue, violet, yellow, orange, white, cream, and pink. It was almost as if the flowers had captured the tiny prisms of light.

Some flowers were large and showy, others delicate and fragile, all a delight to the senses, their perfume scenting the air. As Gilliad knelt down to bury his face in the blooms that had sprung up at his feet, he once more heard the voice of The Creator as He blessed His handiwork so that seeds would grow from the plants, and so the seeds would sprout and form new plants and fill the earth with beauty and fragrance.

And all became calm as evening descended upon the earth.

Darkness had only just begun to fall and Gilliad had only just settled down at the foot of his tree when the calm was shattered by a loud clap immediately above his head. He ran from under the large canopy of the tree, and as he looked up at the sky towards the direction of the noise, tiny bursts of light began to appear; first hundreds, then thousands, millions; stars too many to count, sparkling and twinkling brightly. The once dark empty space had become illuminated in a stunning blanket of light: tiny pinpricks of distant galaxies flung by the power of the Creator into the far reaches of the universe.

A cool, marbled, pale blue moon now touched the earth with its gentle glow, casting shadows of the trees over the earth and touching the ripples on the lake near Gilliad's tree with silver. He remained standing for a long time. There were others standing in groups nearby, but no one spoke. Eventually, he lay on the grass under the splendour of the night sky and slept: a long peaceful sleep, filled with dreams of colour, of light, and of love.

Morning came. Gilliad stretched and opened his eyes. He shut them again quickly, opened one small slit and then the other, shading them with his hand as a brilliant orange sun rose from the eastern horizon to welcome the morning, bringing radiance and warmth to the day and giving order to time.

Gilliad stood and stretched, arching his back. He stood for a moment more, leaning against his tree and gazing at the sky, his hands on his hips. Others were already making their

11

way around the lake and he could also see small figures dotted across distant hills and valleys.

Climbing the nearest hill, he surveyed all directions. He shut his eyes tightly and spun around, almost losing his balance. Opening his eyes again he shrugged his shoulders and set off to explore in the direction he had just come from.

'Good a place as any,' he muttered to no one in particular and, of course, no one answered him.

All day he climbed hills, large and small, walked through forests, deep and cool, skirted around lakes, scrambling over the rocks around the edges, and explored caves, dark and mysterious. Sometimes, he just sat in the lush grass and looked around him or lay on the ground gazing up at the clear blue sky. More than once, he knelt by a bubbling stream and cupped his hands, dipping them into the cool water and drinking the refreshing pure liquid.

He skimmed smooth pebbles over the surface of a crystal-clear lake, counting as the pebbles jumped and skipped: three, four, five times. Sometimes, he enjoyed the company of fellow explorers sharing in the wonders of a new frontier. But most of the day, he was content to explore on his own.

As evening fell again on the earth and the sun slowly slipped out of sight, he made his way back to his tree by the lake, and he lay back on the grass and watched as the stars, one by one, began to shine once more and the moon again bathed the earth with its light.

A mist rose from the water and settled on the new leaves, covering them with dew and trickling into hollows in the flowers and down the stems, soaking into the soil. And the flowers nodded their heads as they went to sleep, rocking gently in the fragrant warm breeze of the night air.

Gilliad, enjoying the peace, the calm, and the quietness that satisfies and refreshes after the fullness of day, slept soundly by the lake under the moon.

But ... the Creator was still at work.

As the sun rose and the dew on the ground began to dry, Gilliad sat up and yawned. He rubbed his eyes and yawned again, stretching his mouth wide and taking in a great gulp of the crisp morning air. He had been awakened by music of a sort, but it was unlike the music of the angels in the sanctuary.

He slowly opened his eyes and stretched his arms high, tilting his head back. He was about to launch into a third yawn, but his yawn was cut short. He jumped to his feet and pivoted on the spot once, twice, his head still tilted backwards, his mouth still open, the yawn now forgotten. Above him the sky was teaming with creatures in flight. Their cacophony was almost deafening as they flew up to the clouds and soared around the treetops. Everywhere there was life and colour. Everywhere there was noise and movement.

Dainty birds were fanning their tiny wings as they balanced on the petals of flowers and dipped their beaks into the nectar-laden centres. Bright showy birds rustled the leaves, swooping and diving, foraging for berries and tender shoots. Large majestic birds glided high in the blue sky, their wingspan rivalling the spread of Gilliad's still outstretched arms. Two raucous white birds with yellow crests on their heads devoured nuts with their strong hooked beaks, their heads jauntily on one side.

Birds with long legs gracefully strode around the lake near where Gilliad stood, stopping every so often to stoop and peck at things unseen in the shallows of the water. He threw one a red berry plucked from a bush next to him and there was a sudden frantic flapping of wings as several more water birds swooped down to the morsel. He laughed and repeated the berry toss several times, each time attracting more.

He stopped. Something had caught his eye. He bent to pick up a tiny feather which had drifted from the sky. He turned it over, brushing it against his cheek and across his lips. He sneezed loudly and a bird on a nearby branch took flight. He threw the feather into the air and watched it dance from side to side as it fell.

He wandered closer to the edge of the lake and sat down on a large flat rock. Two black birds with emerald green neck feathers and bright orange beaks were weaving in and out between the tufts of reeds that were growing near the edge.

As he sat watching the birds, he saw that the water now teemed with life too. Tiny fish, their silver backs flashing in the sunlight, darted in and out of the reeds playing games. Larger fish swam further out in the depths of the lake. Occasionally, one broke the surface of the water, leaping high into the air, its tail and fins flapping frantically.

Tiny insects skimmed the surface of the water. Other insects with jewelled wings also hovered over the water, their fine transparent wings vibrating.

Gilliad watched, fascinated, as a bright orange beetle with tiny black spots alighted on his hand and crawled along his arm, tickling as it scurried through the fine hair – a world in miniature. He placed his finger in front of the tiny creature and it changed direction. He tried again. This time, the creature stopped in its tracks. It put one tiny leg on the large obstacle blocking its path, then it scurried up Gilliad's finger and continued its journey along his other arm.

And once more Gilliad heard the voice of the Creator blessing these creatures – His handiwork – so they would fill the earth.

The birds dispersed, their symphony blending as they spread into the sky in all directions and Gilliad again set off to explore, this time in a different direction.

Around every corner he found new delights. He was, by nature, curious, and he lifted, he turned, he examined; smelling, tasting, touching; some things only once. Must remember that, he found himself thinking, on more than one occasion.

Towards sunset, Gilliad found himself in a valley, cool and shady, amongst tall trees whose canopies spread over clusters of palms and lush ferns. Here the air was permeated with a rich damp earthy smell, and every so often Gilliad came across a waterfall or a babbling, laughing brook where the water cascaded over rocks sending a fine spray over the ferns on the banks.

He followed a path which, after some distance, led him between two large boulders. He sat down on a soft patch of ground which was covered in thick moss. With his back against a cool bare face of rock, he watched as the darkness descended, listening to the sounds of birds as they settled into the trees for the night, and to the quiet dripping of moisture that had collected on the leafy ferns and now fell onto the surface of the rocks.

Drip … drip … drip.

He ate the fruit he had collected along the bank of the stream and then lay down on his back, his elbows bent, hands clasped loosely behind his head. He shut his eyes and, lulled by the forest's gentle sounds, drifted off into a pleasant sleep.

But … the Creator was still at work.

Morning came and Gilliad was puzzled. Again. He could hear noises: scurrying noises, screeching noises, grunts, low growls, the movement of leaves and branches, of little rocks displaced and clattering down the sloping surfaces of larger rocks. He rolled onto his side, propped himself up on his elbow, and looked around, trying to place each sound.

He felt a nudge in the small of his back. He grunted and rolled over and came face to face with something round and furry. Little black eyes stared back at Gilliad from a solemn brown face, and a pointy nose twitched as it sniffed at the ground and then sniffed at Gilliad's face.

'Hello little fellow,' said Gilliad, putting out his hand. The tiny creature nuzzled its nose into the big hand. 'Where have you come from?'

The ball of fur looked intently at him but it did not

answer.

Gilliad picked some of the deep purple berries that were growing on a bush next to the rock and offered them to the little creature. After a few sniffs, it took one in its tiny paws and sat back on its haunches to nibble it, all the while its eyes fixed on Gilliad.

Gilliad placed the rest of the berries on the moss in front of the furry ball and watched as it ate its fill. Once finished its meal, it turned and scurried off into the undergrowth.

Gilliad leapt to his feet and took off in pursuit. He dodged branches which bent low along the banks of the little creek, weaving and winding his way along, trying not to miss his footing on the slippery banks. He ran fast, but it didn't take long before he admitted defeat and the furry brown ball had disappeared under a blanket of ferns.

Gilliad sat down next to the water, panting and laughing.

Once he had caught his breath again, he stood and followed the creek back the way he had come the day before. Occasionally, he caught a glimpse of other creatures: some in the trees, some in the undergrowth, others drinking the cool water of the creek, unconcerned at his passing.

He came to the edge of the forest and out into the brightness of the sun. In front of him stretched a large clearing dotted with shady trees and he sat down under one of them and looked about him.

The Creator certainly had a sense of humour, he thought, as he watched two nimble creatures with long tails and arms as they tumbled in the treetops. They were screeching and calling to each other and swinging from branch to branch throwing and catching nuts and berries and making sport of trying to drop nut shells onto an angel who was leaning against the trunk of one of the trees. Occasionally, he threw them back, which only added to the delight and enthusiasm of the creatures.

A furry creature, almost motionless, hung lazily by its

long sharp claws from a nearby branch, one eye open, watching the show with apparent disinterest. With one slow motion, it swung one arm across to another branch slightly further away from the commotion and resumed its half-slumber.

The Creator's designs were unusual but practical. Gilliad watched as a tall animal with long legs and neck reached effortlessly into the high canopy of leaves. It pulled off a small leafy branch with its long dark tongue.

He caught a glimpse of something that ran past him so fast it was almost in flight – a blur of orange and black. There were animals with smooth, tough skin, some with fur, and others scaly or wrinkled.

The Creator designed for beauty. Gilliad was amazed by the incredible variety of colours and intricate patterns: stark black and white stripes; rich black fur that glistened in the sun with an almost bluish sheen; mottled patterns in browns and creams; and stark white.

'Well, that's going to show the dirt,' he observed to no one in particular as a white-furred animal lumbered off in the direction of a copse of trees.

Gilliad had just reached out his hand to stroke the long ears of a curious temporarily-white ball of fluff that had begun to sniff around his feet when the blast of a horn split the air and, just as suddenly as he had found himself deposited on the solid mass beneath the heavens, the earth retreated beneath him.

Chapter Two

Gilliad once again found himself in the sanctuary. He was standing in a massive portico near the entrance where he had first come in. The flight back had been swift. The earth had retreated beneath his feet, and almost in an instant his feet were on the solid, cool marbled white floor.

He would just have to get used to that, he thought.

After a few moments, Gilliad realised that an archangel had begun to speak to the celestial gathering. He strained to hear. '… but for now, go. Explore. Enjoy. This is your home.'

The throng began to disperse. Gilliad looked sideways at those near him wondering what he had missed. He shrugged his shoulders. Can't get into trouble if I just do what they are doing, he thought. Another thing he would have to get used to: paying attention.

He wandered slowly towards the opening of the portico. He could hear the sound of rushing water. It seemed to come from somewhere beneath his feet – beneath the temple – and he looked down and lifted his feet one at a time, looking at the soles of his sandals. They were dry.

The temple was built high on the plateau of a hill. More of a mountain than a hill, thought Gilliad, as he began to descend the massive stone steps. He paused on the third step and a sudden rush of air entered his lungs. His eyes widened as he took in the view. He realised that, although this was the second time he had descended these steps, it was the first time that he had looked beyond what had immediately surrounded him: the stone floor, the steps, his own feet.

He stood for some time, just looking. He was barely aware of the other angels as they passed him on the step, only of what he could see: the garden of the King.

Between the massively thick stone walls which shone and glittered with a bronze, almost translucent sheen – walls that seemed to stretch on forever – there were gates which shone luminously, emitting a gentle pearly glow. Gilliad could see the gate where the Son had stood before their sudden descent to the great ball of matter below, and he thought again of the privilege of bearing witness to the first days of the earth.

Gilliad had thought that the earth below was incredible; perfect. And it was. But now that he beheld the sight before him, he realised that the King's garden was exquisite, beyond description. In fact, the earth and the memories of what he had witnessed in the moments of Creation seemed somewhat faded now in comparison.

Everywhere Gilliad looked there were paved streets which shimmered golden in the light, almost as if they were fluid. As far as the eye could see, there were lush gardens, trees, grassy meadows, birds, and jewel-like butterflies skimming the petals of flowers; everything a reflection of the Designer – the Master Craftsman.

The garden was sculptured, full of graceful archways, vine-covered bowers, fountains, places for reclining, places designed for contemplation and reflection, and places for gathering and sharing with others. Although in the part of the garden that Gilliad could see from the steps there was symmetry and a sense of order compared to the somewhat wild, untamed beauty of the earth, it occurred to him as he surveyed the garden and beyond, that the Designer had based His earthly Creation on this garden in heaven.

Gilliad felt that he could stand on the stone steps forever and not grow weary of the view. This spot, he mused, he would return to again and again. With this thought in mind, he continued his journey down the steps and into the garden of the King.

The garden teemed with life. Above him, countless birds and butterflies flew, swooped, and glided: small and beautiful, graceful in their flight. Gilliad amused himself for several moments in an attempt to catch a butterfly. It seemed to be teasing him just out of arm's reach. It spun circles around his head and then suddenly shot up until it hovered above the treetops. Gilliad leapt into the air and hovered close to the butterfly, his arm outstretched. He smiled as it gently settled on the tip of his finger.

'Ah, there we go, little one. See? I mean you no harm.' He let himself drift down again and the butterfly flitted away, back to the tops of the trees.

Gilliad examined a tiny creature which had alighted on his wrist. Its body was striped in a fine fur of black and gold. Its delicate wings vibrated so fast they were almost invisible. He blew on the tiny creature and followed its flight to the trunk of a nearby tree. Inside a crevice he could see many more of these little creatures, all busy, their wings humming as they flew in and out of the hole. He dipped his finger into some sticky amber liquid which he found in the hollow of the tree trunk and drew it out. He licked his finger and closed his eyes.

As he leant against the tree listening to the hum of tiny insects, he gradually became aware of another sound. It was like the sound he had heard as he had begun his descent from the temple portico, only gentler, quieter. He followed the sound to the end of a pathway and stopped in his tracks, his sight arrested by a glittering river. It cut its track through the centre of the garden, and the water near the edges trickled over the pebble-lined shallows and danced and bubbled around the larger rocks which broke the surface where the water was deep.

Insects skimmed the surface of the water where it was calm, leaving little ripples as their tiny legs and wings brushed the surface. Birds with long thin legs waded through the shallows, their graceful necks wobbling. Large white birds glided slowly passed, dipping their heads and necks into the cool water then tipping their heads back and shaking a fine spray of droplets from snowy white feathers.

The water that flowed through the garden came from under the temple mount; from the Father's throne. A river of life, thought Gilliad. Everywhere, life from life. And the One who has life in Him – who is life – has given that life to me. And Gilliad knew that his life was a gift: a gift that demanded nothing in return. And yet he knew in his heart that he would give everything: love, trust, obedience.

He dropped to one knee and scooped up some of the crystal-clear water in his hand. He tasted it. It was like the water on the earth. Pure, refreshing, life-giving. It cooled his tongue and he splashed some water onto his face, laughing in delight as his skin tingled, shivered.

He stood near the edge of the water, looking up and down the banks. All along the river grew the most magnificent trees. In fact, although the entire garden was abundant in beauty, it seemed that these trees and the river beside which they grew were the most beautiful part of the whole garden – the centre of the garden – the rest of the landscape giving the appearance of being designed to draw one back towards these trees, this river of life.

The trees that lined the river were laden with fruits. The colours of the fruits were in hues of purple, orange, yellow, and red, all at varying degrees of ripeness and size; many of them ready for eating, others holding the promise of future enjoyment.

The fruit of one of the trees hung down inches away from Gilliad, and he reached up and pulled off a perfectly-shaped smooth ripe globe and bit deeply into it. He sat down in the soft grass, his sandalled feet dangling in the water, savouring the sweetness of the juice, the softness of the flesh.

Leaning over, he trailed his hand slowly through the water. As the ripples subsided, he took in his own reflection for the first time. His hair was a dark chestnut colour with tumbling curls which almost reached his broad shoulders. His face was fair and smooth; his jawline chiselled and strong.

He peered closer at his reflection and turned his face first one way and then the other. Hmmm. Eyes match hair. Not bad, not bad. He smiled at himself, revealing two rows of white teeth, small pieces of purple now stuck to several of them.

He leant back on one elbow, enjoying his fruit, taking in the sights, the sounds, the smells; contemplating this small part of what was to be his home: the home he would share with the Father, the Son, his fellow angels.

He picked another fruit; this one yellow and different in flavour, but just as sweet and even juicier, if that were possible. He bit into it, letting the juice trickle down his chin. He finished the fruit, lay back in the soft grass, and closed his eyes; enjoying, listening, feeling.

If this was to be his life, well, it was alright! Yes, indeed. Alright.

Gilliad jumped. He had been startled by a hearty greeting. A loud voice had come from somewhere behind him and he sprang quickly to his feet, slipping on the grassy embankment. He grabbed a clump of reeds and scrambled into a half-crouching, half-kneeling position.

'I'm alright,' he said. He looked up at the owner of the voice.

'No need to get up, my friend,' said the voice, with a laugh.

The voice, Gilliad could now see, belonged to a rather tall, powerfully-built angel whose shock of fair hair fell in unruly waves, framing his bronzed face.

'Sit, sit,' the angel grinned. 'Oh you are sitting ... sort of.' His emerald-green eyes twinkled. 'I am Latorius. Perhaps we will be in the same league.' He reached for some fruit.

Gilliad nodded, resuming his seat on the grassy bank. 'Perhaps.' He had heard some talk of leagues from a few of the other angels he had met on the earth. 'I am Gilliad,' he said, by way of introduction. He paused for a moment, considering his new friend. 'Our mission. What do you know?'

'Ah ... that, I believe, will be revealed in the Father's good time. The Father is patient,' assured Latorius. He finished his fruit, toss the seed against the trunk of the tree and looked at Gilliad. 'I see you did not get very far,' he said with a laugh. 'Come. I will show you the splendour of heaven.' He swept his hand in a wide arc as he spoke.

If Gilliad had intended to linger by the water a little longer, he certainly couldn't now. Latorius' enthusiasm was contagious and Gilliad felt compelled to follow. He popped the last of his piece of fruit into his mouth, grabbed another two – one for each hand – and followed his new friend back along the path.

Latorius laughed. 'That's probably not necessary. There is food everywhere.'

Gilliad looked at his hands. He shrugged his shoulders. He wasn't going to risk it.

The King's garden seemed to stretch as far as the eye could see, perhaps even further. They meandered along a path lined with blossoms and the rich scent permeated the air as they brushed past them.

Gilliad and Latorius greeted many of their fellow angels as they explored; some in groups, others alone. The camaraderie was easy, and they stopped to exchange greetings many times, sharing their discoveries with each other, shaking hands, slapping each other on the back, or simply nodding in acknowledgement as they passed. There was much to explore and Gilliad and Latorius found new delights around every corner: natural beauty, architectural splendour, and perfect design.

They wandered the paths and wide streets, sometimes taking to the expanse above the treetops and exploring their home from the air. They travelled for miles in every direction, and yet Gilliad had a feeling that they had really only just begun to discover the delights of heaven.

And Latorius was right. Everywhere there were things to eat. In fact, he had deposited the two pieces of fruit soon after they started their exploration in favour of consuming … well … who knows how many different types of edible delights. He had soon lost count.

They eventually alighted near a large marble fountain which was set in the centre of a spacious alcove. The alcove was surrounded by trellises, heavily covered in a winding vine. Its leaves were a glossy deep green and the branches generously peppered with heady white blossoms which hung upside-down. They watched as a tiny brown and white speckled bird flitted between each flower, its long sharp beak reaching deep into a flower as its wings vibrated, suspending it between the petals.

They made their way over to a stone bench close by the fountain with the intention of enjoying a leisurely pause in their exploration. A gentle spray of water from the fountain splashed onto the stones and a tiny green creature basked at the foot of the fountain under an arch of coloured mist.

They had been there only moments when a horn sounded in the distance: a long steady blast, like the one that had summoned their return from the earth.

Gilliad looked up at his companion.

'It is time to go, my friend,' said Latorius. 'We must gather at the meeting hall.'

They moved swiftly through the air towards the sound

of the horn, taking in all that passed below them. From above, the garden was awash with colour, the water shimmering and sparkling; everywhere vibrant with life.

They alighted on the pavement next to The Great Hall and joined the closest group. Gilliad ventured a look around him at his comrades: those who would share his home. They were like him in many ways, and yet each one had features that were unique.

Their hair was in various shades of black, brown, and auburn, some golden, others almost white. The colour of their eyes ranged from deep blue to sparkling green, or hazel to dark brown like his own, with many variations in between. Their colouring was varied too: some pale, some with olive complexions, some bronzed, others dark-skinned. Even their voices were distinct: some deep and commanding, some quieter and more reserved, others jovial – much like Latorius – their eyes twinkling to match their voices. They were individual; each one special; each one known and loved by the Father.

Like Gilliad and Latorius, the other angels were dressed in robes of white linen. The robes hung from their shoulders, pulled in at the waist by a wide sash, and flowing from the waist down to the knee. The sashes they wore around their waists were of many different colours, signifying their ranks and denoting their league. Their robes had no sleeves, displaying well-defined muscles that flexed with every movement.

Their hands were strong and yet gentle, able to crush or caress, and the muscles in their calves rippled as they moved, powerful and purposeful in their step. Their feet were clad in a thin, flat sandal with narrow bands that wove in criss-cross fashion up the leg, ending just below the knee.

Approaching the closest entrance, Gilliad took in as much as he could see of The Great Hall. It was well named: an imposing structure with huge solid doors along each long side. There were intricate carvings inlaid into the panels on the outer sides of the doors and he squeezed his way into the group examining the panels on the door they were about to enter.

The first carving was of the earth covered by water: the moment the Creator called into existence space, time, and matter – the elements of the physical universe. The second carving depicted tiny figures stretching out into the far reaches of the universe: figures that faded into dots – angels suspended in space. It was the moment that the Creator breathed into being the hosts of heaven. Gilliad's beginning. He peered closely at the carving as if looking for a dot sporting wavy chestnut hair.

'Me,' he declared solemnly, tapping a finger on one of the dots.

'Ha,' snorted Latorius. 'I think not. Wrong eye colour.'

Some of the carvings were of the creatures, the plants, and the flowers that he had seen on the earth: the story of The Creation. But there were other carvings depicting scenes that he did not understand, figures he had not seen, events he had not witnessed, and it intrigued him.

They passed through the open door and found themselves in the wings of the ground floor of the hall where they were immediately directed towards another doorway. Gilliad followed Latorius up a short flight of stairs, two at a time, to the second tier of The Great Hall where they were greeted warmly by one who introduced himself as Arkellus.

Arkellus, like the other archangels Gilliad had noticed, wore a wide gold sash and stood an easy head taller than the angels. Many of the archangels had coloured bands around their upper arms, and Gilliad saw that Arkellus wore a band that matched the sashes around the waists of both himself and Latorius.

Gilliad inclined his head in greeting. The archangels were of the highest rank of celestial beings. Their presence commanded respect and their counsel was rich in wisdom.

Arkellus returned the gesture. Like his fellow archangels, Arkellus, at the same time as holding authority over those angels of the lower orders in his charge, was humble. He knew that his role of authority went hand in hand with great responsibility and, although he would command, he would also lead by example.

Arkellus gestured to a table close by. At each place was a small piece of parchment, and in elaborate flowing script was written the name of each guest. Gilliad and Latorius took their seats. The seats had almost filled and The Great Hall was humming with easy chatter and laughter. Although there were thousands upon thousands of angels, The Great Hall easily accommodated the throng.

Gilliad looked over the edge of the balcony at the floor below them. At the end of the building closest to the sanctuary there was a raised white marbled platform, and in the centre of the platform there was a large seat, carved and solid, like those around the tables. This one was set with precious stones which glistened and shone, giving the seat a regal and dignified air. The chair of a king.

There were raised platforms at many levels around the interior of the building, all furnished with large rectangular tables and highly-polished timber chairs. On the ground floor there were also a number of long tables, each surrounded by ornately-carved chairs.

All of the tables in the hall were set with fine white linen and golden candlesticks, intertwined with fresh vine leaves. Each place was set with golden goblets and fine polished silver. The centre of each table held huge platters of food, and Gilliad recognised many of the fruits that he had discovered and tasted on his exploration of the King's garden. There were large pitchers of wine, baskets overflowing with breads in all shapes and sizes, numerous bowls of colourful sauces, and vessels of freshly picked herbs, ground spices, and fragrant oils for dipping. The aroma that met Gilliad's nostrils made his mouth water and he breathed deeply, letting his breath out in a long satisfied sigh.

As the last of the angels took their seats around the

numerous tables lining the tiers of The Great Hall, some of the archangels – those without a coloured band around their upper arms – took their places at the tables on the ground floor in front of the marbled platform.

Arkellus made his way to the head of the table where Gilliad and Latorius had been directed, and he nodded again to his fellow guests.

The archangels had no sooner taken their seats when the air of noisy excitement gave way to a quiet hush and they stood again, turning as one towards the marbled platform. The angels followed their lead, thousands of chairs scraping the rough flagstone.

And again, there was silence.

Gilliad heard the voice of the Son before he saw Him: the voice, quiet and gentle.

'The love and peace of the Father be with you all,' He began. 'The Father invites you to eat your fill of this bountiful feast and celebrate the gift of life He has given you.'

And thousands upon thousands of angelic voices in perfect harmony filled The Great Hall with a melody of praise and thankfulness. The feast, Gilliad realised, was secondary. Had the food and drink been absent from The Great Hall, nothing would have been missing, for in the presence of the Son all else seemed to fade.

The Son held out His hands to the assembly and the archangels resumed their seats, followed by the angels.

The feasting began.

At each table there was laughter: the easy banter of friends who had always known each other. They shared in the discoveries they had made in the seemingly unending expanse of the King's garden, and marvelled at the power they had witnessed at the creation of the earth. They shared in the excitement and anticipation of things to come and the joy that comes with having a purpose, with being a part of something of great importance, great significance.

Gilliad looked around him at the food. He was not sure if it were possible but he intended to sample everything. He took a sip of red wine from the goblet in front of him, and the sweetness made his mouth and jaw tingle as he swirled it around. Its aroma was fruity but heady, like the scent of the blooms that grew by the fountain.

He plucked a tiny purple globe from a vine. He popped it into his mouth and bit down on it. It burst and released its soft sweet pulp and juices into his mouth. He sampled a delicate flaked bread. He thought it tasted a little like the honey he had found in the hollow of the tree. It was made of numerous soft white layers which he was able to peel off so thinly they were almost transparent. The bread seemed to melt on his tongue.

There were clusters of nuts: some earthy and some creamy; berries of many different kinds: some sweet, some tart and tangy – purples, blues, reds, and golds. He dipped a juicy-looking red berry into a nearby bowl of creamy-brown sauce and popped it into his mouth whole, even the stalk and a few green leaves, and closed his eyes, savouring the delicate contrasts of fruity freshness, the crunch of tiny seeds, and the creamy decadence of the sauce.

'Mm mmm,' he murmured between mouthfuls to nobody in particular, 'I could never tire of eating this.'

Eventually, Gilliad, whilst falling far short of his goal to sample all the delights that were laid out before him, was satisfied that he had had his fill, and he sat back contented and looked around.

Each tier of The Great Hall was designed so that, from every table, one could see the marbled platform. Each tier extended all the way around three sides of the building and there were steps at intervals between the levels.

The fourth wall, which was devoid of tiers, stretched high above the marbled platform and was inlaid with coloured glass windows in a myriad of designs, patterns, and pictures which let in shards of coloured beams.

Windows on every floor on the other three sides also let in the light, giving the hall a gentle glow and encouraging one to take in the view of the garden from many vantage points. Gilliad turned in his chair and looked out the window behind him. In the distance, he could see the imposing structure of the sanctuary and the sparkle of the river as it danced its way from under the temple mount and meandered between the tree-lined banks.

He wondered how far the river went; where it led to. Did it lead back to the sanctuary? He thought it probably did. He had noticed there was a river flowing under the sanctuary from the opposite side to the steps. Was that the same river? he wondered. Did it go out from under the throne and return again? They had certainly not seen the end of any river during their explorations.

So rapt was he in his thoughts, Gilliad had not noticed that, as the feast had progressed, the Son had left the marbled platform and had made His way along the tiers, greeting an angel here, encouraging another there, blessing each and every one.

Sensing a lull in conversation at his table, Gilliad turned from his view of the sanctuary and the gardens to find himself looking into the face of the Son; into the eyes of eternity: the eyes of wisdom, of love; eyes that saw deep into his very soul.

He felt his heartbeat quicken within him as the Son spoke directly to him. 'Gilliad, I have chosen you to do great things for me. You will be a gentle protector, a faithful servant.'

The Son gently laid His hands on Gilliad's head. 'The blessing of the Father be upon you.' And the warmth from those gentle hands spread through Gilliad; throughout his entire being.

For perhaps a short time, perhaps forever, Gilliad was unaware of anything around him. He sat with his eyes closed until, eventually, the hum of voices found their way back into his awareness and he once more became part of the scene in front of him.

The feast had finished. The Son was addressing the celestial assembly.

Chapter Three

The excitement among the angels was palpable; the air charged with anticipation.

Arkellus, as the leader of the legion of which Gilliad and Latorius were a part, had now joined them outside and had led them to a large courtyard adjoining The Great Hall. The archangels had stayed behind long after the angels had poured out through the doors, and Gilliad had paced the entire length of the wall several times, questions milling around in his head.

Arkellus' imposing stature needed no elevation, and as his voice carried across the courtyard all became quiet.

'I am Arkellus,' he began. 'I have much to say.'

There were six thousand angels in each legion, Arkellus explained. Each legion was under the command of an archangel. There were many legions, each with different coloured sashes around their waists. Gilliad, like those around him, wore a deep blue sash – the colour of the roaring tossing oceans far below on the earth – and he looked around with interest at those in his legion.

There were a number of archangels who did not command a legion, but who had been put in various roles of authority. The angels around Gilliad's table had shared what they knew of these elite archangels and Gilliad had caught the names of a few in this group.

Michael, strong and warrior-like, would function in some kind of protective role, the details of which were yet to be revealed. Gabriel, noble and wise, would be a messenger – one who would announce and proclaim, conveying the words of the Father to the assembly and His messages from heaven to earth – a position of great trust and responsibility. Lucifer, beautiful to behold and with a voice that captivated, would lead worship in the sanctuary. Abaddon, his presence commanding and his stature imposing, would be one of the keepers of The Great Hall. And there were many others, all with missions and responsibilities.

The archangels were to meet often in The Great Hall for instruction and guidance. Here they would receive messages conveyed to them by Gabriel. They would then pass these messages on to their various charges. When necessary, they would hold court to discuss any issues that arose, to put forth their ideas and suggestions, and together plan what their response or reaction would be. All members of the group would be listened to. Each archangel's opinion would be considered. Gabriel would convey their decisions to the Son who would have the final say on each decision. On occasion, the Son would preside over the council meetings.

All angels were required to participate in strength and endurance training out on the large fields of heaven, on the open expanses of the earth below, as well as in the space surrounding heaven and earth: exercises that would build their trust in each other, as well as improve their skill, speed, and agility. Gilliad absorbed this information with interest and again ventured several sideways glances at his companions, sizing them up for future challenges. The competition, he decided, was more than worthy, and he looked forward to pitting his strength and skills against theirs.

There would be many occasions when they would gather again in The Great Hall. There would be celebrations, feasting.

Now that, thought Gilliad, patting his stomach and

attracting an elbow from Latorius, sits well with me.

The doors of the sanctuary – the Father's house – would always be open. Sometimes they would gather to worship together; at other times they could approach the throne alone. The Father would always welcome them.

A horn blast sounded.

'We must go now,' said Arkellus. 'Come.'

They left the courtyard near The Great Hall, forming a long procession that wound down the paved street and followed the pathway towards the river. They crossed over a wide bridge and Gilliad looked down into the clear water. A long flash of orange darted out from under the bridge, its scaled shiny body curving this way and that as its tail effortlessly propelled it through the water. Two large white birds with long curved necks followed, floating gently downstream with the current. He wanted to stop and look, but now was not the time.

They headed once more towards the gate close to the temple, and then they stood waiting while the many legions of angels, led by their commanders, took their places in the courtyard.

Finally, the gate opened and they poured through, almost in a fluid motion, like a white waterfall spilling over the edge of a cliff.

Heaven seemed as if it had moved closer to the earth, and as Gilliad passed through the gate he could even make out some of the features of the earth: the mountains and valleys, rivers and streams. As he came closer, he could see tiny figures moving around: animals and birds.

They descended rapidly and alighted directly below in a beautiful garden.

'Yessss.' Gilliad managed to remain on his feet. He held up his hands and glanced around. No one had missed their footing. 'Oh. Alright then.'

He looked around him. The garden, at least from where he was standing, seemed to be closely modelled on the King's garden, for it had a decidedly cultivated air.

He looked at Latorius. 'Shall we?'

'Indeed we shall.'

They could hear the sound of running water and they followed the direction of the sound down a narrow pathway that led through the garden. There was something orderly and refined about the garden: the placement of the flowers, the neat rows of trees that lined the winding pathways, the carefully placed rocks; some with large flat surfaces perfect for sitting or reclining on under the canopy of trees or beside the river.

There was a large spreading tree with ripe fruits on it in the centre of the garden, and Gilliad recognised it as the same tree that grew beside the river in the garden in heaven. The tree had massive roots which spread down to the water, and where it touched the water it gave off a brilliant shimmer of light, sending tiny prisms of colour dancing into the stream. As the prisms spread in an increasing arc from the roots of the tree, they were carried in the current down the stream, continually refreshing the water with life.

The river divided into four branches which wound their way in all four directions to the edges of the garden and continued out of the garden, through the lush land of Eden, then on through other lands, joining with other rivers, streams, and waterfalls before flowing into the sea, taking the life-giving water to all four corners of the earth, then returning again to the river in Eden; passing through the garden; passing once more through the roots of the tree of life.

Gilliad sat down by the river. He toyed with a stick, twirling it on his fingertips, balancing it, throwing it in the air, and catching it. Latorius joined him, occasionally taking a swipe at the stick as it fell towards Gilliad's hand.

'Do you know what we are to do here?' asked Gilliad.

'No more than you do, my friend,' Latorius replied, snatching the stick mid-air.

'The Creator has finished, has he not?'

'That I could not say. If I had the mind of the Creator, I would perhaps have an answer. But I do not. It is as if all that He has done on the earth has been in preparation for something, though. I have a feeling that it is not for our sake that He has created the earth. Our home is in heaven. It seems as if we are waiting for something,' observed Latorius.

They lay back on the grass, talking about the events they had witnessed.

Evening would soon fall upon the earth, and already the birds had begun to make their way to the tops of the trees where they would roost for the night. The air was cooling and the sun had sunk close to the horizon, giving the sky a purplish-pink hue.

Gilliad could hear the chirrup of insects hidden in the reeds by the water. He carefully parted a clump and watched, fascinated, as one of the insects rubbed its legs together to make the sound. It suddenly jumped at his face startling him and he fell backwards providing momentary entertainment as he lay sprawled on the ground.

As he lay looking up at the sky, he became aware that a hush had fallen over those around him and their attention was no longer focussed on him. He sat up. Latorius was standing on a rock and he climbed up and joined him.

There was a newcomer to the garden.

Gilliad could see that the figure was similar to himself in form and shape.

There was a ripple of whispers throughout those gathered. A man.

Arkellus now joined them, standing on the adjoining rock. He had come from the same direction as the man and the Son and what he had seen, he shared with them, his voice low.

According to Arkellus' account, the Son had formed the man from the dust of the ground, weaving together bones, muscles, and sinews. Then the Son had knelt down and lifted the man's head and brought the man to life with a breath – His breath.

'Then he has a spirit?' Gilliad asked. 'If he has life, he must have a spirit, mustn't he?'

'Indeed he must and he does,' Arkellus said. 'It was the Lord's own breath that formed the man's spirit within him. And he has a soul. His spirit flowed from his heart throughout his body imprinting it and forming his soul.'

'Then he is like us?'

'Sort of. But he is also physical.'

'The dust.'

Arkellus laughed. 'Yes. The dust.'

There was something familiar about the man. Gilliad thought hard. He knew he had seen the man before. But he couldn't have, could he? He frowned. Then it came to him.

'He's the ...' started Gilliad.

'I know,' interrupted Latorius.

'... figure from the panels,' Gilliad announced in a loud whisper, as if to inform anyone who may have been in any momentary doubt.

The man looked around him with wide eyes. A bird flew close to him and he shrank back. The Son held out His arm and called the bird and it flew from a branch and landed on His hand. The man reached out his hand and the bird hopped onto it. He stroked its feathered back and it sang for him: a throaty warble with notes that rose and fell. The man tried to sing with the bird but it flew back to the branch.

The Son took the man and led him by the hand and showed him things and told him things and gave him things: things the Son had created for him. They paused together every few steps, touching, examining. The Son spoke gently to the man with words too quiet for Gilliad to hear. And the man smiled and nodded and many times he laughed. And the Son laughed too.

Gilliad watched the man's face as he ate the fruit that the Son pulled from the trees and gave to him to try. The delight of discovery was still fresh in Gilliad's mind and his mouth watered, despite his belly still being full from the feast in The Great Hall. The Son reached up and plucked a ripe fruit from the tree of life. He gave it to the man to eat and the man closed his eyes as the sweet juice trickled down his chin.

The light was getting low and the first star of the evening had already announced the arrival of the night. A quietness had now descended over the garden and the man lay down and slept, the Son by his side.

And the Father blessed the man, blessed mankind, and He rested from all His work.

Gilliad had dozed on and off throughout the night, occasionally propping himself up on one elbow to look around. The garden had been bathed in silvery-blue moonlight and all was peaceful, with only the occasional sound of a bird rustling in the trees and the gentle babbling of the water as it flowed over rocks and pebbles. The man had not stirred.

As the sun began to rise in the eastern sky and the garden began to come alive again, Gilliad rose from his spot and set off down one of the many paths that led from the small clearing near where they had slept.

He stopped at a large clumping plant and broke off several wide leaves. He rolled them into cone shapes and tucked them under his arm. It didn't take him long to find a decent helping of fruits, berries, and nuts and the makeshift vessels were soon full. He found a hollow in a tree which had honey in it and he broke off a small piece of honeycomb and chewed it as he walked, sucking the sweet amber liquid out of it and spitting the waxy remainder into the bushes. He returned to his spot by the river, his arms full.

'For me?' Latorius looked at the supplies with interest, one eyebrow raised. He had still been asleep when Gilliad had left and had then lingered by the river. He had been splashing his face with the cool water on Gilliad's return.

'Ah ... well ... not exactly,' said Gilliad, 'but I guess I could probably spare a small morsel of something for a friend.'

'Too generous of you.'

'Humph,' retorted Gilliad, stuffing a handful of berries into his mouth as he arranged his supplies between them on a rock.

'Next meal is on me,' promised Latorius.

Gilliad laughed. Getting a meal was a pleasure to him. Eating was an even bigger pleasure.

Halfway through the meal, Gilliad remembered the man. He scrambled to his feet, climbed onto the flat rock, and peered in the direction of the large spreading tree where the man had lain down to sleep the night before.

He stood there open-mouthed.

'What?' Latorius joined him and his mouth also dropped open.

Parading past the man was a long procession of all kinds of creatures.

The man was saying something and Gilliad strained to hear. Some of the words were muffled, but others carried on the breeze and he could just make them out.

'... giraffe,' the man called out as the long-legged, long-necked creature Gilliad had seen the day before paraded past. 'Kangaroo ...' and Gilliad watched as a brown-furred creature with pointy ears and small front paws bounded by the man in great leaps, propelled through the air by its powerful tail.

The next in the parade took its time, sauntering along slowly, its large hard patterned shell shining in the morning light. 'Tortoise,' said the man. 'And lemur,' he added, for the tortoise had picked up a passenger along the way.

There was a quick succession of animals after that, as the tortoise had caused a bit of a bank up. 'Rhinoceros ... hippopotamus ... tiger ... zebra ...'

And the Son watched the face of the man as each creature presented itself.

Gilliad and Latorius sat back on the rock and continued their meal. The man was still at his task when they had finished and they could not see the end of the procession. They wandered down to the river to drink once more from the refreshing cool water before setting off to explore the Garden of Eden.

The sun had passed the middle of the sky when they returned to the spot where they had eaten. The animals had just finished their parade and the last of them – a large lumbering creature, which they had only caught a quick glimpse of as they came back into the clearing – had just disappeared into the bushes.

The man had patted them, laughed at their antics, marvelled at their unique design, and named them all. They, in turn, had nudged him with their noses, sat in his hands, perched on his shoulder, and slithered over his feet.

But among them, no suitable companion could be found for the man.

Adam – for that was his name – was different to the animals, for he was made in the image of the Creator.

The Son and the man were still standing near the tree and as Gilliad and Latorius watched, the Son placed His arm around the man's shoulders and, as He touched the man's forehead, Adam's body suddenly went limp.

Gilliad looked at Latorius with wide eyes. Latorius shrugged his shoulders.

The Son gently laid the man on the ground. He placed his hand on the sleeping man, opened his side, and took out a rib. He closed up the side of the man with His hand and the flesh was restored.

The man slept on.

Gilliad again looked at Latorius.

'I don't know,' whispered Latorius.

Why would the Lord do this? Gilliad wondered. Was not the man perfect? Complete? Had there been a mistake made in his construction? One too many ribs perhaps? He shook his head. Everything in Creation was perfect. There must be another reason.

And there was.

As they watched, the Son began to fashion something out of the rib. In the hands of the Master Sculptor, something beautiful was taking shape beside the sleeping form of the man.

The masterpiece completed, the form unfurled itself, stood, and inhaled slowly.

The Son stepped back and waited.

The man stirred. He slowly sat up. He tucked both legs under him and sat for a moment rubbing his eyes. Then he put his hands on the ground and got to one knee. He reached out to steady himself against the trunk of the tree and then stood. He stretched and yawned, taking in the coolness of the evening air.

Out of the corner of his eye he caught a movement. He turned sharply, almost losing his balance, and found himself face to face, eye to eye, with the most beautiful sight in the whole garden. He stepped backwards, stumbled again, and righted himself. The woman laughed, throwing back her hair.

Gilliad watched the man's face.

The man was impressed. Gilliad was rather impressed himself.

The woman was a lot like Adam, but there was a softness about her – a daintiness. Her skin glowed. Her long wavy hair fell down in loose ringlets over her shoulders and her back. She was curvy where Adam was angular and muscular. Her lips were full, soft, and a deep pink, and she smiled at Adam, her husband, her eyes twinkling.

Adam reached out his hand and stroked her cheek. He ran his other hand down her soft silky hair, all the while looking into her eyes.

'Eve,' he whispered.

And the Lord blessed them – husband and wife.

The angels returned to heaven. They all had stories to tell – things that they had seen and heard while in the Garden of Eden. The mission of the angels was becoming clear: they were to minister to man.

'All of us,' Gilliad had mused when he first heard of this, 'to minister to two of them?'

Arkellus had joined them in the courtyard. He had overheard Gilliad and laughed. 'That might sound a little over the top,' he said, 'but just you wait. After Adam was created, the Lord blessed mankind so that they would fill the earth. Then we will see just what an enormous task this mission really is.'

'When will we return to the garden?'

'When the Father sends us. The man and his wife need time alone, time to enjoy the closeness they will share and time to explore the garden together. That is their home. The man and women must learn to tend the garden and take care of it,' explained Arkellus. 'The Lord has given them a purpose too.'

'Is it true that there is a tree that they are not to eat from?' asked Gilliad. Talk of the garden always led him to think of food. 'I overheard Lucifer saying this as we were walking through the courtyard. He said he had heard the Lord God saying to Adam that he could eat the fruit from any of the trees in the garden except one.'

'Yes,' replied Arkellus. 'That is true. Man can eat from any of the trees except the one in the middle of the garden. It is the one set back a little from the bank of the river; the one opposite the tree of life.'

'And if he does eat the fruit from this tree?'

'Then he will die,' Arkellus stated bluntly.

Gilliad looked up. 'But the man and the woman have eternal life, don't they?'

'That's true. But eternal life is a gift. The man and the woman only have this gift of eternal life through the Spirit of the Father. If they were no longer connected to that life, they would no longer have eternal life.'

'But how would eating the fruit of the tree cause them to be cut off from the life of the Father and the Son?'

Arkellus nodded slowly. He had only just begun to understand this himself, and he took his time to order his thoughts before responding.

'It's like this:' he said. 'Man was created with an open heart. It is only through his open heart that he receives life from the Spirit. But his heart will only remain open to the Spirit of life through faith in the Creator. Just as you and I have a choice whether to put our faith in the Creator or not, so does man. If man chooses to go his own way his heart will close. He will have chosen to depend only on himself, but in doing so, he will become disconnected from the Spirit of life – the gift of eternal life that he has only through the Spirit of the Father.'

They made their way to a seat near the river and they sat for a while as Gilliad thought about what Arkellus had said. So this was eternal life, he thought. Surely man would realise the folly in rejecting that gift. And yet … if rejecting the gift wasn't a very real possibility, the Creator would not have needed to warn the man, would he.

'So if man chose to disobey and eat the fruit, then he would be cut off from the life of the Father and the Son; he would lose the gift of eternal life,' said Gilliad, after several moments. There were many things that he did not understand.

'Yes. But obedience is a choice, love is a choice, trust is a choice. Man must be allowed to choose.'

Gilliad nodded, understanding most of what Arkellus was saying, storing away the rest. He had much to contemplate … later. There was still exploring to be done … a lot. And eating … definitely more eating.

While the evenings and mornings passed on the earth and the man and the woman lived in the garden together and tended it, heaven was busy.

Most of the angels had not been down to the earth since they had witnessed the creation of mankind and they had spent much of their time out in the fields of heaven. Gilliad had learnt many skills, each of them designed to improve agility and strengthen muscles.

He had learnt to use a sword and, over time, had risen to the challenge of taking on some of the archangels, although he was always out-skilled. Nevertheless, he thought, it served to strengthen his resolve to be the best he could be.

There were horses that roamed the open fields near where each league trained and Gilliad had, after numerous attempts, managed to mount a horse with a flying leap without ending up on the ground on the other side. Latorius had cheered him on as he practised until, finally, he had landed smack in the middle of the horse's back, triumph lighting up his face, surprise on the face of the horse.

'We did it,' he exclaimed. He bent forward and rubbed the horse's nose.

'And now while the horse is running,' challenged

Latorius.

'Ha,' grinned Gilliad. 'Easy. I will show you next time. Don't want to wear the horse out!'

'Right,' said Latorius, laughing. 'Always thinking of the horse.'

There were also fencing lessons. These were designed to teach them to be light and quick on their feet, and in this Gilliad excelled. There were strength and resistance exercises: rolling large round stones up hills, lifting boulders, pushing against trees and against each other. Gilliad's muscles had developed considerably, and he was now able to roll a stone twice as large as when they had first started training.

There were also skills to master in the space that surrounded heaven and earth, and the further he explored, the more Gilliad was amazed at the vastness of the universe. The galaxies seemed to be infinite in number; the glow of tiny pinpricks of light appearing to stretch on forever.

During their training, the angels learned to trust their leaders and obey their commands. Arkellus was tough on them. He would work them hard but would always give praise where it was due. He asked nothing of them that he was not prepared to do himself.

Many of the activities they did involved putting their trust in their training partner. Latorius oozed confidence and was easy to trust. They had had a few mishaps but nothing too serious.

Once, they were racing in pairs up a hill carrying a boulder, side-stepping in unison, Latorius counting them through each pace, when Gilliad had dropped his end of the boulder and it had careered down the hill. But they had made swift flight to stop it before it had rolled more than halfway down, thus avoiding having to start all over again. They lost that race, of course, coming last, much to Latorius' disappointment, and Gilliad was to be reminded of it often.

Another time, the sword fighting had become so intense

that they had to be split up by Arkellus. 'Right! Practice over, time out!' he had yelled over the clash of swords. 'Back to the river. Cool off.'

Gilliad was disappointed at the abrupt end. He had almost managed to get Latorius over the line. A couple more strategic moves, a bit more fancy footwork, he thought, and he was sure he would have won.

'Just as I was about to let you win,' Latorius had said with a sideways glance at Gilliad.

'What? I almost had you beat. You would have been finished if we had not been cut short,' panted Gilliad, as they jogged along the path that led to the river.

'Nah,' teased Latorius. 'I was going easy on you. Just about to start trying, I was.'

'Sure you were. I saw the look in your eye when Arkellus broke it up ... pure relief!'

'You just keep telling yourself that, my good friend. You just keep telling yourself that.'

'Next time you won't be so lucky,' promised Gilliad.

'Challenge accepted!' Latorius replied, with an on-the-run low bow.

It was not all work, though, and they gathered in The Great Hall many times. They enjoyed each other's company, swapping stories, encouraging one another, eating together, and at these times, The Great Hall would echo with hearty greetings, laughter, and, of course, the clink of silver.

There were also quiet moments when they would wander down to the banks of the river, sit on the cool grass, and relax. And there they would talk. They would listen. They would learn.

Sometimes the Son would come and sit among them and they learnt about love, not just by what the Son said, but from what He did. For the Son was love and the Son showed them the love of the Father.

Gilliad was drawn to this love. He needed this love like he needed the air he breathed; even more so. It was the same love that drew him to the sanctuary where he would worship in front of the throne, bowing low before the Father, kneeling in silence, or singing praises to the One who held his life in His hand.

There were times when all of the angels and archangels would gather together in the sanctuary and the worship, led by the archangel Lucifer, was powerful and moving, and Gilliad felt that there was no place he would rather be than worshipping at the feet of the Father.

And the love that he received from the Father and the Son flowed out from Gilliad to those around him and from them to him; for they were family.

Below on the earth, the man and woman tended the garden. They cared for and loved the creatures that shared the garden with them. And they were content. They had food, water, shelter; every necessity, every comfort, and they were happy in each other's company.

They ate from the bounty of the garden. They ate the fruit from the tree of life and they drank from the cool clear waters of the river that flowed through the roots of the tree.

In the cool of the evenings, they enjoyed the company of the Son as He walked in the garden with them, speaking to them of the things of heaven and earth, and of love. And they would sit at His feet and worship. Their adoration was pure, their trust complete, and they loved Him.

And He loved them.

One evening, Lucifer watched from the shadows of the garden, not content to be confined to the heavens.

And he was jealous.

He wanted that for himself: to be loved, to be worshipped

... adored.

And desire began to build in his heart. It started as a tiny seed. And it grew. And his heart became bitter, discontented, envious. And his heart closed, shutting out the gift of life ... of love.

And a plan began to form in his mind.

Part Two

Chapter Four

They gathered once again in The Great Hall, but this time the atmosphere hung heavy. There were no hearty greetings; there was no laughter; just quiet urgent whispers as they took their places around the tables.

Gilliad looked at those around him and they looked at him. No one was sure exactly what had happened. Arkellus was at his usual place at the head of the table, but he had not looked up at them since they had arrived and his lips were drawn in a tight line.

Some of the angels looked different, Gilliad thought. It was as if there were something missing – an absence. He did a quick inventory. They still wore what he wore: the robe, the sandals, the sash. Their hair was still the same; not as nice as his, he thought, but that hadn't changed.

He sat and stared at one of them several tables away. The angel felt Gilliad's gaze on him and looked up. It was then that Gilliad realised: it was the eyes. Of course. He should have noticed that straightaway, now that he thought about it. Their eyes were dull and lifeless; dark even. The pupils were large, dilated, as if trying to let in the light. It was as if the windows of their souls had somehow closed out the light.

Their skin, too, was different, as if it had somehow lost

its radiance. And their faces, which were once full of the joy of life, had become sullen, almost expressionless.

There were many like this; thousands even. The angel looked away.

Gilliad looked down at the archangels on the main floor below. Even a number of them had taken on this demeanour. Their heads hung down, their shoulders drooped. Amongst their number were Lucifer and Abaddon. Lucifer, however, held his head high – jauntily – a smirk on his face. He was quite animated, Gilliad noticed, almost jovial, and he turned and twisted in his seat, this way and that, as he talked to, first one, then another archangel close to him.

As Gilliad watched, Lucifer pushed out his chair and stood. He slowly made his way to the marbled platform, stopping to pat a few archangels on the back, saying a few words to others. Gilliad heard him laugh a few times, but the laugh sounded hollow.

He mounted the platform and walked slowly to the centre and sat himself down on the large carved chair. There was a collective gasp, which only served to fuel his pride, his arrogance. He cast his eyes over those gathered in front of him before lifting his head to take in his audience on the high tiers around the hall.

He waited for a moment until all was quiet. He waited a moment more.

He again looked around at the gathering; first at the lower floor, then at each of the tiers.

'My friends,' he began, after clearing his throat, 'you may well wonder why I am addressing you. And I say to you: why not? The Son is not the only one with something worth listening to.' A murmur rippled through the assembly and Lucifer held up his hands to quiet them.

He swallowed and then coughed several times before he began again. 'I stand before you today ...' He paused briefly, and there was a collective snigger among some of the angels,

'… to put before you a choice. Many of you have already chosen to follow me and you will not regret it. To the others, I am graciously giving you a chance to join them.'

There was another murmur amongst the gathering: one of confusion.

'Make me your leader,' he continued, 'and together we shall rule the heavens and the earth.'

He forced his voice to project in an effort to reach the top tiers. It had become raspy and he coughed again. 'I ask you: why should we obey the Father?' he was now yelling, his voice hoarse. 'How do we even know that He created us? Were any of you there to see it happen? No. What proof is there? Why should we take His word for it? Couldn't we have just appeared without being created by anyone?'

Again there was a murmur throughout the hall, some agreeing, others protesting.

'What is he saying?' whispered Latorius. 'That we just happened to come into existence? That the Father did not create us?'

Gilliad looked around. Those who had lost the light in their eyes were nodding eagerly at the speaker, hanging on his every word. Others were frowning and looking sideways at those near them.

'Surely no one could fall for this blatant lie,' whispered Gilliad.

Lucifer continued in a now thick voice. 'Why should we obey the Father? Don't we have a choice? Must we just blindly follow? You can be the master of your own destiny! Stand up for yourselves! Take control!' he shouted, spittle flying out of his mouth.

'Follow me and I will show you a better way! Give me your love, your trust, your obedience.' His breath now came in short bursts and his face was quickly greying.

Gilliad watched in disbelief as those angels whose eyes

were dull, whose skin had lost its radiance and taken on a sallow appearance, one by one got to their feet. Others, including a few of the archangels, began to join them and Gilliad noticed that, immediately, they too lost the light from their eyes and their skin took on a dull lifeless tone.

Those who stood had now begun quietly clapping, but spurred on by their leader, they became louder. They began stamping their feet, making a low rumbling noise. Then one of the archangels, whom Gilliad recognised as Abaddon, began calling out, 'Lucifer, Lucifer, Lucifer,' until all of them were shouting out the name of the traitor and the walls of The Great Hall reverberated with the sounds of rebellion.

By this time, about one third of the angels and a handful of archangels were on their feet. Gilliad sat back in his chair shaking his head, his hand over his open mouth. He could not believe how easily so many of them had been deceived. He could not believe how quickly they would give their allegiance to another; to a pretender.

Lucifer now rose from the chair, his dull lifeless eyes darting here and there. His dry lips were curled in a half-smile, half-snarl, his nostrils flared. His face, once beautiful, was now marred and ugly. There was no beauty in it, only deceit.

'Leaving love is no victory.'

The voice – a whisper – cut through the abrasive sounds of rebellion.

As one, the assembly became silent. There was no movement. It was as if the very moment had frozen and life had been suspended. The eyes of the entire gathering had shifted their focus to the left and behind the traitor.

Lucifer turned his head and found himself face to face with the Son.

His mouth gaped. He faltered briefly, then seemed to regain his composure. 'Your seat,' he said, gesturing with a sweep of his hand.

There was silence.

The Son remained where He was.

Lucifer's composure again seemed to be crumbling and he turned back to face the assembly. Those standing were still frozen to the spot, their faces pale.

Gilliad watched the face of the Son. He neither conveyed contempt nor anger, but in His eyes there was sadness. It was almost as if He had known that this moment would come, Gilliad thought.

The Son addressed the silent assembly. 'You have all made a choice of the heart. Some of you have chosen life, some death. Those of you who have chosen the way of death have made your own path. You have chosen to follow Lucifer, but it is the way of evil and there will be consequences. It is also the way of death.'

As the Son spoke, Gilliad noticed that Lucifer had again edged closer to the carved seat.

'You knew the love of the Father,' the Son continued. 'You will never know that love again. In the Father's house you were safe, comforted, protected. You will never know that protection again. To you have been revealed the glories of heaven, but you have chosen the path to eternal fire. This is no longer your home.'

The Son raised His arms over the assembly and a noise came from the direction of the sanctuary. It grew louder and louder, becoming a roar as it approached The Great Hall, and a look of terror spread across the faces of the angels and archangels who were standing, their faces reflecting the horror that had now dawned in their sinful hearts.

Gilliad looked at Lucifer. The look of bravado, of pride, had been replaced by uneasiness, and the uneasiness was quickly replaced by pure fear as he began to realise the consequences of what he had done. His mouth gaped but no words came out and he began to crumble as his knees gave way beneath him.

The sound had become almost deafening and the

building shook. Suddenly, a powerful wind – the Spirit of The Most High – roared through the windows and doors of The Great Hall, whipping around the interior and picking up the rebels as if they were weightless, and the wind flung them mercilessly, scattering them into the darkness, down to the earth below.

And all was quiet.

The remaining angels – those loyal to the Creator – slowly made their way out of The Great Hall. No one spoke. There was no need for words. Each one knew what the others were thinking, and their faces were grim.

Gilliad made his way down to the river to think. He had a favourite place – a place where he liked to relax and unwind after training exercises – and that was the spot he headed for now. He sat down on the grassy bank.

Latorius joined him, easing himself down next to his friend. They sat for a while in silence, the quiet soothing sounds of the river slowly easing their troubled minds.

After a while Gilliad spoke. 'How could this have happened? How could they do this?' He shook his head and let out a shuddering sigh.

'They were given freedom just like you and me,' said Latorius. 'In time they will come to understand that we are the ones who are free.' He leant his elbow on his knee and rested his head on the palm of his hand. 'You know, that could just as easily have been us disobeying; being thrown out of heaven.'

'No!' Gilliad cried. 'I could never betray the Father or the Son.'

Latorius smiled at his friend. 'That is probably what some of them thought, but that is exactly what they did. They were witness to the splendour of heaven, the unveiling of Creation, and the power of the Creator. They were given the same love, the same choices as you and I.'

'I will never allow my heart to turn away from the Father.'

'I know,' Latorius said, quietly. 'I know.'

They sat for a while, each with his own thoughts, as life went on around them. The river still flowed, birds still sang, fish still swam amongst the reeds. It was as if nothing had happened. And yet, somehow, everything was different now.

At the sound of Arkellus' voice, they scrambled to their feet.

The Archangels had remained behind in The Great Hall after the angels had filed out. They had sought counsel with the Son and then had left to seek out those of their league who had remained faithful.

They nodded respectfully to the leader of their league. His face was grim. He motioned for them to resume their seats and then sat down beside them. They were joined by several other angels with dark blue sashes, eager to find out what had happened after they had left the hall.

None of their league had fallen from grace, Arkellus reassured them, and that gave them some measure of comfort. But there was nothing that could be done to bring those who had rebelled back under the grace of the Father. Lucifer had chosen to rebel against his Maker, thinking that he might set himself on the throne in place of the Father; be worshipped in the Father's place. Those who had followed Lucifer had each made their choice, and for them, it was too late.

Lucifer was now to be known as 'Satan', no longer worthy of the name the Father had bestowed upon him.

'S ...' Gilliad could not bring himself to say the name.

Latorius smiled at his friend, Gilliad, gentle protector, faithful servant. He knew his friend would always be worthy of his name. He just knew it.

'Will the rebels still share our home?' one of the angels asked.

'No. They have been banished from the King's garden, from The Great Hall, and from the expanse within the walls of heaven,' Arkellus said. 'With one exception,' he added. Gilliad, who was listening intently to Arkellus, sat up straight at this. 'There will be times when the Father will summon them to appear before the throne. And then, they must come. Whether they like it or not, the whole of creation is under the command of the Father and all are answerable to Him. That includes the rebels. That includes Satan.'

There were murmurs of agreement at this.

They had many questions for Arkellus, which he answered patiently and with as much detail as he could, given what he had been told in The Great Hall.

'Will the rebels always be free?'

'No. Their days of freedom are numbered.'

'Will they ever be banished forever from the heavens and from the earth?'

'Yes. They will one day be judged and sentenced. A time is coming when they will be banished from the face of the earth and from the heavens above. Only the Father knows the day, the hour.'

'But what will happen to them then? Where will they go?'

'They will be imprisoned deep within the earth where they will never again see the light of day.'

'But where?' one asked. 'There is surely nowhere for them to go.'

'Within the earth there is a fire that burns continually,' explained Arkellus. 'It will now be prepared to one day receive the devil and his angels. They have forfeited the glories of heaven for an eternal fire. Abaddon, whom you will recall was a keeper of The Great Hall, will, from this time on, remain at the entrance to the shaft that leads down to the abyss where the lake of fire is until the rebels face judgement – his punishment for following Lucifer. He now holds the key that unlocks the shaft.'

The small gathering sat for some time in silence.

'What if they escape?' asked Latorius, after a time. 'What then?'

Gilliad had been thinking the same thing.

'It will not be possible. After the rebels have been judged and sentenced, the shaft leading to the lake of fire will be sealed for all eternity. Once it is sealed, there will be no escape. What God closes, neither angel nor man can open.'

'But for now the rebels are allowed to roam freely everywhere apart from heaven?'

The questions had come full circle, but Arkellus was patient.

'Yes, anywhere.'

'What about on the earth?'

'Yes, even on the earth.'

Gilliad looked up in alarm. Surely he had missed something. 'But what about the man and woman?'

'The man and woman are protected by the Father for as long as they remain in Him; for as long as their faith and trust is in Him; for as long as His Spirit remains in their hearts.'

And Gilliad remembered what Arkellus had told him as they talked about the man and woman after they had returned from the garden on the earth: 'Obedience is a choice, love is a choice, trust is a choice,' he had said. 'Man must be allowed to choose.'

And Gilliad's heart ached as he remembered the innocence in the eyes of the man and his wife.

After Arkellus had left them, they had sat by the river for some time talking about what had happened. As they sat, they had noticed that the gentle music that continually drifted from the sanctuary had become louder. They rose to their feet and began to make their way along the paved streets towards the courtyard. As they mounted the steps, they were joined by many more angels, each of them drawn to worship. The sanctuary was quickly filling, and they entered through the portico and took their place amongst the throng of angels and archangels.

The singing and the worship were one, blending in their hearts and being outpoured through their beautiful voices. Never before had they sung with such passion. Even with their numbers diminished, they were complete.

They needed to worship. They were made for worship. And Gilliad found himself kneeling down before the Father, his face bent low, his arms outstretched on the cool marble. His awareness of anyone but the Father faded as he let the peace of the Father's house, of the Father's presence, wash over him.

The sanctuary emptied and Gilliad followed those in his league out to the training fields. He felt refreshed and his strength was renewed after being in the sanctuary. Training was just what he needed at that moment. He had energy to burn; steam to let off.

He eased himself into a jog – a slow jog at first – then built up speed. He always liked to warm up before testing himself with any of the challenges.

Latorius caught up to him. He enjoyed Latorius' company and, after the obligatory 'three ... two ... one', they raced each other between fences, hurdled over obstacles, and dodged between trees, sometimes Gilliad leading, sometimes Latorius.

They worked on mounting and dismounting the horses. Gilliad, to his delight, could now mount a horse mid-gallop – quite a feat according to Arkellus, who occasionally ventured over to give encouragement and offer advice.

Gilliad loved riding the horses and did this any chance he got. Most of the time, the horses just galloped on the field, but like the angels and archangels, they were also able to take to the air, and Gilliad enjoyed the challenge of trying to remain seated whilst the horse he was mounted on tossed and leapt and bucked, free of the restraints of the ground below.

Sometimes they had chariot races, both on the ground and in the air, and the heavens echoed with shouts of: 'Hup! Hup! Faster, faster … whoa,' and the horses would snort and whinny, shaking their magnificent manes and long silky tails, almost as competitive as their riders.

Like the swords of the angels, the horses and chariots were able to appear as fire, and it was a common sight to see flames streaking across the darkness of the universe as they raced each other.

Sometimes, when they were practising with swords, Gilliad and Latorius would take to the air on the horses, crossing swords with each other until either one of them fell off or they agreed that the match was over and neither one was the victor. But both were as determined as each other to be the victor, so rarely did they agree to quit.

This time, the sword fighting was on the ground on foot. On these occasions, the horses were usually behind the fence grazing on the lush green grass that grew in the fields. Occasionally, they would look up at the swordsmen, their attention arrested by a sudden cheer. Then they would return to the task at hand … eating.

This time, before they started their training, each of the angels was instructed to choose a sword and a strong belt with a scabbard attached to the side. Every other time they had trained, they had just been given any sword from the collection that was used to practise with, but this time was to be different.

There were different lengths, thicknesses, and widths in the collection, and they were expected to be proficient in the use of each style. This time, they were informed by the angel whose responsibility it was to look after the swords, they were to keep the sword. It would be their own.

They made their way over to the weaponry – a large lowset building, the entrance of which opened onto the training fields. They walked along several corridors of swords; all of them placed in perfect rows from the floor to the ceiling; all of them polished and sharpened, ready for action.

Gilliad selected a medium-length wide silver sword. As he slowly turned the handle over in his hand feeling its weight, he noticed that the handle was engraved. 'Gentle protector, faithful servant,' it said, in flowing script. His eyes opened wide. It was the words of the blessing the Son had spoken to him.

He stood for a while as other angels came to select their swords and he watched as each of them, on examining the handle of his sword, had the same reaction. He placed his sword carefully in his scabbard and joined Latorius.

Latorius' sword had the words 'loyal and trustworthy' engraved on it, and he held himself erect, shoulders back, as if to somehow convince Gilliad that the sword spoke accurately.

'Perfectly matched,' said Gilliad, nodding as he read the words.

They assembled on the field in their various leagues and waited quietly as the archangel in charge of sword training gave instructions to the other archangels about the session they were about to commence.

Before long, Arkellus returned to the front of their group and spoke to them. 'My friends, up until now, training has been aimed at strength, agility, balance, and control. You have all worked hard, rising to each challenge, building trust in your fellow angels, and working together as a team. Well done,' he said, looking around.

'You are all aware of the events that have just taken place,' he continued. 'We have not seen the last of the rebels.

In fact, you will cross paths with them again and again, both in the air and on the earth. They will try to thwart the Father's plans at every opportunity and you must be ready to defend yourselves, to fight if necessary, and to protect mankind.'

He looked around at their solemn faces. 'There will be times when you will work alone, and times when you will work with your partner or even with your entire battalion. There will be wars waged in the heavenly realms and on the earth below: wars that man will know nothing of. You must be prepared. The rebel forces are strong, but their numbers are only half of ours. They will believe that they can defeat us, but they have been deceived by the evil one. The Lord is with us. The victory will be His.'

A rousing cheer went up from Gilliad's league and he looked around at their determined faces. They were angels of honour. Their loyalty was to their Maker.

Gilliad needed to be alone to think. He headed to the river and wandered slowly along the winding path that wove in and out of trees and bushes. He paused every so often to pick a few berries or to scoop up some of the crystal clear water in his hands to satisfy his thirst. He climbed the steps of the sanctuary and sat for a while, surveying the beauty of the garden. The Great Hall was in view – an imposing structure – its windows glinting in the light, reflecting the colours around them.

As he sat on the steps thinking about The Great Hall and the events that had recently taken place in there, he remembered the carvings on the doors. He had seen some of them the first time they had been into The Great Hall as they gathered outside the massive doors. There had been carvings depicting The Creation; carvings that told of the earth being formed and moulded into shape. He had seen figures that he now recognised as the man and the woman, but when he had first looked at those carvings, they had made no sense. It was as if the scenes could only be understood after each event had happened.

He got to his feet, leapt down the steps, two at a time, and headed for The Great Hall. There were other angels walking together in groups of twos and threes and he greeted them as he passed, but he did not stop. He reached the door where he had first entered The Great Hall and paused in front of the large wooden structure.

He examined the carvings of The Creation again. They were intricate and detailed – the work of a master craftsman. He touched the smooth curves and ran his fingers into grooves and hollows and along perfectly straight lines. The pictures were even more detailed than he had remembered. Every petal, every leaf, was individually carved, and Gilliad could even make out the tiny legs of insects and the fine stems and delicate stamens of flowers.

. Gilliad wandered further along the building and stopped in front of the next door. He found a second carving of angels suspended in flight. It was very much like the one on the first door – the beginning of his existence. He had seen this one before, but he now took a closer look at the angels' faces. The faces were distorted, the robes twisted. The rebellion, he realised. The memory, still fresh, made him shudder.

His eyes moved to the next carving: a scene back on the earth, in the garden. The man and woman were standing next to a tree. The woman was eating fruit picked from the tree, and she was giving another piece of fruit to the man to eat. There were little creatures in the carving, Gilliad noticed: birds flying overhead, tiny furry animals near the trees in the background, and a serpent nestled in the branches of the tree.

And Gilliad thought of the man and the woman on the earth in the garden, and he smiled to himself as he remembered the look on the man's face the first time he laid eyes on the woman.

And every other time, he realised. And every other time.

Chapter Five

The man and his wife woke with the first rays of the morning sun. Their day began slowly as they unfurled from their slumber on the soft bed of bracken under the overhang of rock. They had fallen asleep, Adam with his arm around Eve's shoulders, Eve against his warm body, her head on his shoulder, the sounds of the garden and the gentle glow of the moon for company.

They lay side by side, hand in hand, enjoying the crispness of the air and watching the pale sky as it came alive with birds as they left their night abodes and took to flight.

Adam rolled over to peer over the edge of the flat rock, propping himself up on his elbows and supporting his chin with his hands. Tiny creatures had already begun their foraging, and Adam watched a small bushy-tailed possum sitting on its haunches holding a ripe orange fruit in its paws. The skin was tough, but the creature easily tore into it with its sharp claws and teeth, turning it expertly over and over until the skin had fallen in a little pile at its feet. It had no sooner popped the tasty morsel into its mouth when it scampered off into the undergrowth in search of another.

Eve slowly sat up, stretched her arms to the sky, and arched her back. Her long hair now glistened with gold: sun-kissed highlights which fell over her shoulders and down her back. She sat up on her knees with her legs tucked under her and she lay her hand on Adam's back.

Suddenly, Adam leapt to his feet. 'Come, my beloved!' Springing from the rock, he landed lightly on the ground below and extended his hand to his wife.

Eve, once recovered from being startled by her husband's mid-air flight, arose somewhat more gracefully and placed her hand in his. With a swift tug he pulled her off the rock and into his arms, twirling her around and around. She struggled to regain her breath as the air entered her lungs in short bursts between laughter.

After several twirls and one more for good measure, he put her down, but still she hung on to him tightly, her arms clinging around his neck. She kept her eyes closed until her head had stopped spinning and she had regained her balance. Adam stood almost a head taller than her and she tilted her chin and held her head back so she could look into his eyes. She knew he loved her like he loved his own body. He would do anything for her; give anything to her. And she to him.

Adam bent his head down until their foreheads lightly touched. He kissed her on her lips: a slow kiss, cupping his hand behind her head, and entwining his fingers in her soft hair. She was beautiful. She smelt like the warmth of the sun, the purity of the river, the fragrance of the flowers of the garden, and all his senses were heightened with the love that he felt for his wife.

They wandered hand in hand down the path to the river, stopping close to the large tree where its massive roots wound down the bank and disappeared under the cool water. Close to the bank where they had come to bathe there was a plant with glossy green leaves, and from one of its lower branches Adam plucked a large yellow flower which had just opened. He gently tucked it behind his wife's ear, leaving a tiny trail of orange pollen across her cheek.

Adam offered his hand to Eve and they carefully stepped down the embankment and ventured into the shallows of the river until the water came up past their knees. They lowered themselves down into the currents and the water swirled and bubbled under their chins. The water was refreshing: cool enough to awaken the senses but warm enough, at least after a few minutes, to relax in.

The day before, Adam had managed to move a number of large rocks into a rough circle, and they soon moved to this calmer haven where they were protected from the swirling currents.

Adam leant back, balancing in the water with the back of his head leaning on the edge of a large rock, leaving only the upper part of his face exposed. He floated like this for several minutes, his eyes shut, his body relaxed, suspended in his watery bed.

Eve sat upright, her knees drawn up, her arms wrapped around her knees. She watched her husband for a while. Every now and again, a smile would spread across his face and she wondered what he was thinking about. After some time, she slowly pushed herself up onto her hands and knees and slipped over the top of the rock she had been leaning against. Keeping her head low in the water, she moved around the circle of rocks until she came to the rock next to Adam's head: the rock where the flow of water split into two streams and gushed around the outside of their rock haven.

Reaching her hands under the water, she placed one hand on either side of the rock. She dug her toes deep into the soft river bed, anchor herself firmly, took a deep breath, and heaved with all her might, sending a great gush of water over Adam's peaceful face.

Adam emerged from the torrent after several moments gasping and spluttering. He scrambled to his feet and leapt onto the rock next to the displaced one, overbalancing. Regaining his footing, he turned his head to the left, just managing to catch a glimpse of the top of his wife's head as she ducked down behind the rock on the other side and immersed her head in the watery shadow.

Little bubbles rose to the surface and the large yellow flower drifted with the current down the stream, its petals sodden and limp.

Adam stepped onto the other rock and crouched down. He knew his wife could hold her breath for a long time. They had often challenged each other, diving below the surface some way downstream from the tree where the river flowed into a waterfall and the water was deep. Often, she won.

After several moments, the tiny bubbles that had been steadily rising to the surface ceased and Adam lowered his face close to the water where his wife would likely emerge.

Moments later, her head broke the surface and she rose blinking the water out of her eyes and gasping for breath. She shook her hair, spraying Adam with a shower of tiny droplets which clung to his eyebrows and beard. Finding her target, she reach up and threw an arm around his neck and pulled hard, reefing him off his rock and sending him splashing and tumbling into the water. As he came back up to the surface, she pushed herself away from the rock, her arms ploughing a path backwards through the water. But her husband was quick and grabbed her foot, pulling her back. He brought her to him and held her tight in his arms. She laughed and squirmed in his tight hold. Seeing the struggle was futile, she relaxed.

'Resistance is pointless,' Adam said, loosening his grip momentarily.

Seeing her opportunity, Eve launched herself backwards and pulled him under with her again.

The man and his wife lay for some time on the smooth large flat rocks near the bank of the river. It was almost the middle of the morning and the rocks were warm from the sun. They stretched out, allowing the breeze and the warmth of the sun to dry their bodies. The woman's hair cascaded down the edge of the rock on which she lay, and as it dried, it framed her face with little spirals.

'Shall we eat, wife?' said Adam. He held out his hand to his wife and together they wandered back along the path.

When they reached the tree of life, Adam reached out and took two of the lush fruits that hung from the branches, giving one to his wife. The fruit of the tree was a gift; life was a gift, and the man and woman bowed their heads and said a simple blessing over the food.

They stood under the tree and ate. They never gathered the fruit from the tree of life; never stored it; it had never been discussed or decided, they just didn't. The rest of the food was different, though.

They returned to the shelter where they slept and collected one of one of the simple baskets that Eve had fashioned. It was woven from the branches of a low-growing palm, and its leaves had dried, providing a strong support for holding their food. It had two handles made of vines which Adam had attached to the basket, and they held a handle each as they picked the food that they would eat that day.

They wandered the paths of the garden, gathering berries, fruits, and nuts. Eve had become quite adventurous and often surprised her husband with her culinary combinations. She ground nuts, she added honey from the hollows in the trees, and sprinklings of various herbs and seeds. She mixed in fresh fruits and also fruits that she had dried by hanging them on long sticks suspended between branches in the warm sun; at least those that the birds did not help themselves to. They ate well and they enjoyed their food, especially Adam.

Adam had learnt to climb trees and could now negotiate a tall palm tree in seconds and knock down a coconut with precision, landing it with a thud right in the centre of the curved piece of bark he had padded with bracken to cushion the impact. He had also become skilled at hitting a coconut in exactly the right spot with the perfect amount of force so that it split evenly down the centre revealing the sweet white flesh. He had found a rock surface that was perfect for doing this on. It had an indent running along the centre, and when he hit the coconut, the milky juices would flow along the hollow and drain into a vessel on the ground. At least when he remembered the vessel, that is.

A number of times he had proudly presented his wife with a perfectly cracked coconut shell, each side equal, no ragged edges. She would take the shell halves in one hand and she would hold out her other hand.

'The juice?'

'Oh.'

And she would sigh and shake her head at him.

He had fashioned a number of tools out of rocks and sticks, and with one of them he deftly scraped the flesh of the coconut he had retrieved for their breakfast, turning the hard white fibrous flesh into a fine pulpy mound on the rock. Eve mixed in a little honey and ground nuts and shaped the sweet mixture into balls with her hands before pressing them flat on a smooth rock.

While his wife finished preparing their food, Adam tended the fire he had made with twigs and leaves and small logs which he had gathered on their walk. He had a small collection of hard, thin grey stones which he used to make a spark by striking them together. He found that if he did this repeatedly over dry grass and leaves, eventually he could manage to coax the kindling into flames ... eventually. Patience was the key, according to the opinion that Eve had volunteered.

'Man's job,' she had stated simply when he had offered the flints to her to try one day. And that was that.

The sweet coconut cakes were placed on a large leaf and wrapped tightly. Adam laid them in the hot coals he had pushed to one side of the fire, and before long the aroma permeated the air. Several little visitors turned up and watched with expectant eyes.

'If I have to wait, so do you,' Adam said. 'But you'll be lucky if there is anything left this time. Pretty hungry,' he said, patting his belly.

When the cakes were cooked, Adam pushed them off the coals with a long stick and opened the leaves. The steam from the hot cakes rose into the air. There were two circles of woven palm fronds laid out on the grass and he quickly flipped the cakes onto them. He took them to his wife who was pouring fresh coconut milk into two shallow bowls that he had made from the shells of coconuts. This time, he had remembered to collect the juice.

They had accumulated quite a large collection of these bowls, each one scraped free of the fibrous husks that clung to the outside, and they used them for drinking and eating out of and for holding all manner of food and other items: nuts, dried berries, dried fragrant leaves, fresh or dried flowers, even pretty stones found by the river. Nothing was wasted and Adam had found that the coconut fibres made perfect kindling for their fire.

They sat down on the grass, a large leaf between them on which they placed their meal, and they gave thanks for the food.

Adam stole a sideways glance at his wife as she lifted the coconut bowl to her mouth. 'Yes,' he thought to himself with a slight nod, 'a wife who looks good and can cook. I am truly blessed.'

'What are you grinning at?' Eve asked.

'I am just thinking how beautiful you are and how blessed I am that you are here with me.'

'No,' Eve said, shaking her head. 'You are just thinking about your food as usual, not your wife.'

'My dear, you are mistaken,' Adam replied, raising one eyebrow. 'If the whole earth were teeming with women who could cook as well as you, I would still only have eyes for you.'

'Pfft,' was Eve's reply, her mouth full of warm cake, less one crumb which now hung off Adam's beard. She retrieved it and smiled a crooked smile at her husband. 'Like that will ever happen!'

'Be fruitful and multiply,' quoted Adam, raising the other eyebrow.

'Fill the earth,' finished Eve, with a laugh.

Eve gathered the coconut bowls and took them in a basket down to the river. She knelt down and held them one by one in the current, letting the force of the water rinse them clean. She returned to the fire and lay them upside down in a row to dry.

'What are you making, husband?' she enquired, presently.

Adam was sitting cross-legged on the grass holding a dried piece of hollow bamboo. He had made a number of holes in the side and was concentrating on the making of the last hole. He had a sharp thin piece of stone which he had brought back from the river the previous morning, and he held the bamboo tightly between his feet while he twisted the stone around, pressing it firmly as it dug into the timber.

'There,' he announced. 'I think it is ready to try.'

Eve looked at him and frowned. 'Invention number ... what are we up to now?'

Adam snorted. He had lost count. Now that he gave it some thought, had he even counted that high before? He wasn't sure.

He brought the hollow tube to his lips and blew. The noise sounded like the wind that blew through the trees. He moved his fingers on and off the holes and blew harder until his face began to turn pink.

Eve tried to suppress a laugh but failed. 'Um, Adam, that sounds ... ah ... interesting,' she offered, struggling for some appropriate words of encouragement. It was not the first time that he had made something that did not quite live up to his expectations, but she also knew that once he had an idea he was not going to give up easily.

'It should work.' He sat looking at the bamboo, frowning. He turned it over and over then sat looking intently at a spot in the sky. Eve looked up; there was nothing there, of course. She had once questioned his habit of doing this.

'That's the whole point,' he had tried to explain. 'Looking at nothing. That's how you come up with ideas.'

She wasn't sure.

'Wait.'

She waited.

'What if ...'

He jumped up, tore off down the path, and disappeared, leaving Eve shaking her head in his wake. Again. She would just have to get used to his sudden flashes of inspiration, she thought. Sudden everything, come to think of it! Although, what he was up to this time, she could not even guess.

She sat down on the grass by the fire. It was now just low flames and hot coals. She threw a few nuts into the coals and they sizzled and hissed. These would be a welcome meal later that night. She reached behind her and pulled the mat she had been weaving onto her lap. She had gathered several types of palm fronds and was weaving these into a pattern. The leaves were a variety of shades of green – some pale, some darker – and they would make a fine mat to lay across the soft bracken where they slept at night.

She had almost finished weaving the ends of the fronds into the edges of the mat when something made her stop and look up. A sound was coming from the river: a sound that she had not heard before. It was pleasing to the ear and she sat and listened, her hands still, resting on the unfinished mat.

She stood up, placing the mat back on the grass, and

she began to walk along the path following the strange sound.

She stopped for a moment and listened again. The sound was a little like the call of the water birds: the ones that stood in the shallows on one leg. But it was deeper, more melodious. She continued down the path.

As she came close to the river, the music stopped. She looked along the bank.

Adam was sitting on a rock, his hands behind his back.

'Did you hear that beautiful sound?' she asked.

'What sound, wife?'

'It was coming from the river. I followed it here, but it stopped. You must have heard it.'

He gave her a blank look.

'I suppose you were making too much of your own noise, doing whatever it is you are doing down here.'

Adam smiled. He beckoned to his wife to sit down beside him on the rock. He drew the bamboo pipe from behind his back and lifted it to his lips. She saw that he had fixed a small piece of bamboo in the top of the hollow tube and had fitted a piece of reed from the riverbank into it. He had also added a small hole on the underside of the tube.

Placing his fingers over the holes, he took a breath and blew steadily into the tube. A deep low sound came from the bamboo. He took another breath and moved his fingers over the holes. The notes rose and fell as he lifted first one finger and then the other.

A small creature stopped in its tracks and turned its head to watch for a moment before resuming its scurrying. A tiny bird alighted on the rock, and for a few moments added its own melody, taking the high notes of the harmony.

Adam played slow full notes at first and Eve closed her eyes and lay back next to him on the rock. Sometimes, she opened an eye, always to find her husband's eyes on her. She knew he was making the music just for her and she was happy lying there on that rock in the garden by the river with her husband.

Her thoughts drifted and the music and the warmth of the sun made her feel drowsy.

Suddenly, a shrill piercing note snapped her from her slumber and she sat up.

'Adam!' She quickly regained her composure.

Adam's eyes twinkled. The notes quickened. Sharp and fast he began to play.

Well, if it's like that then, Eve thought …

She clapped her hands twice and jumped off the rock and into the middle of the clearing. Twirling and dancing, her long hair flew in a wide arc behind and around her as the tempo of the music increased. Round and round. Faster and faster.

'Keep up with me,' she shouted over the music.

He did. For a while, at least. But before long he could not resist joining his wife in the dance. He leapt off the rock and took her hand in his while still trying to play his flute with the other.

She laughed at his attempts at dancing and playing music at the same time. He soon gave both up. He bowed low and she clapped in delight.

'Try it,' he said, holding the flute to Eve's lips.

She sat back down on the rock until she had caught her breath again, then she lifted the bamboo to her mouth. She placed her fingers on the holes and blew as she had seen Adam do. It made her lips tingle as the reed vibrated, but she managed to make a sound.

'It's not as easy as it looks when the master is playing,' she said.

'Ha. Try again.'

She tried again, this time managing a few notes. They didn't sound too bad, she thought, and she smiled a smile of satisfaction: the smile of one discovering the possibility of the emergence of a hidden talent. 'Will you make one for me?' she asked her husband.

'Well ... I could, I suppose, but it might take me a while. A lot of orders have just come in.'

Eve rolled her eyes.

'Of course I will make you one, my love,' he said. 'We shall play together.'

She smiled. He would do anything for her. She knew it to be so.

'And what colour would the lady prefer?'

Eve laughed. She thought for a moment. 'Surprise me.'

'I will.'

'You do, Adam,' she said, kissing him on the forehead. 'You do.'

He took her hand and opened her fingers one by one. He held her eyes in his and lifted her open hand to his lips and gently kissed her palm. She loved him, her husband.

Evening came and they sat side by side near the warm glow of the fire. Adam had gathered dry leaves and had blown onto them, fanning the coals until the fire had come to life again. He had learnt that it was much easier to leave a few coals from the morning fire to start the evening one rather than having to start the fire all over again. He had found a few small logs and put them on the fire to last until they settled for the night.

Eve warmed the remaining coconut cakes for their supper. 'It is so nice to have some food left over. It saves having to make something new each time.'

'Wife,' said Adam, biting into a cake, 'as usual you are very wise.' He thought for a moment as he chewed. 'Perhaps we should call this food 'leftovers',' he suggested.

'Leftovers,' Eve echoed. 'Yes. I like that. You can expect leftovers again soon then,' she promised. 'Often, in fact,' she added, warming to the idea.

They ate the roasted nuts that Adam had cracked open and heated some water in which Eve had placed some fragrant green leaves. When the flavour of the leaves had steeped for long enough, they sat sipping the warm drink, thinking on their day and listening to the crackle of the fire and the sounds of the night.

The moon had waned to just a tiny sliver peeping through the dark branches of the trees, but the stars shone brilliantly, lighting the dark sky above them.

They finished their drinks and left the bowls by the fire to be washed in the morning. 'Why do today what you can put off until tomorrow?' was one of Adam's favourite sayings; not necessarily one that Eve agreed with, but on this night she did.

Hand in hand they walked back to their shelter under the overhanging rock.

While Adam had gone to look for logs for the fire, Eve had finished the mat and it was now laid out on the soft bed of bracken.

'It's beautiful,' he said. 'Almost too pretty to lie on.' He squeezed her hand.

'Well,' Eve replied, 'you can stand all night if you prefer.' She was pleased that he had noticed her handiwork straightaway though.

He laughed and pulled her down onto the mat. 'Not if you are lying down.'

They lay on their mat in the darkness, side by side, hand in hand, content with their own thoughts.

'Ahh ... truly a blessing is a wife who knows how to make a man comfortable,' thought Adam, as he shut his eyes.

'Ahh ... truly a blessing is a husband who notices

even the little things,' thought Eve, and she sighed a sigh of contentment as she snuggled in to Adam's side. It was where she came from; where she belonged. 'Goodnight, my love,' she said quietly. 'Goodnight.'

There was no reply; just a quiet snoring. Eve smiled to herself and sighed again, kissing Adam lightly on the cheek. Listening to her husband as he slept by her side, she closed her eyes and soon drifted off to sleep.

Chapter Six

Eve woke a little after dawn. The sun had risen just high enough in the pale sky for its rays to begin to penetrate the dense foliage of the garden, and the mist still lingered in sunlit stripes that reached from the canopy to the ground. She rolled onto her back and reached out her hand, feeling the spot where her husband always slept. It was empty.

She sat up and looked around. Adam loved to rise before the dawn and often sat down by the river enjoying the still, quiet garden.

At her feet there were flowers, and she picked them up, smelling their perfume: a small bouquet, just picked, with the dew still beading on the petals. Most of them had narrow white petals with yellow centres, but there were a few larger blooms providing contrast in the cheerful arrangement. The larger flowers had tiny thread-like projections protruding from black centres and wide petals of red that were soft and velvety. Tiny feathery ferns were poked in amongst the flowers, their tips sticking up just enough to tickle her nose as she brought the bouquet up to her face. She undid the fine thread of vine that was wound around the bouquet and leant over to place the stems in the bowl of water next to the mat where they slept.

'Stop! Don't move!'

Her hand jerked and water splashed over the side and pooled under the coconut shell.

'Adam! Don't do that ... unless you want water all over your side of the mat,' and she made to throw the remains of the contents of the bowl in her husband's direction. He ducked. 'Where have you been anyway?' she asked, as she arranged the flowers.

'Out.'

'Out where?'

'Just out.'

'And did you meet anyone new?' It was their standard morning joke.

'As a matter of fact ... no.'

Eve laughed. She finished arranging the flowers and stood up to shake the dropped leaves off the mat. 'You'll be wanting some food, I suppose,' she said, reaching for two bowls.

Adam held up his hand and she stopped, her hand poised above the bowls. 'Stay right there.' He leapt up onto the rock in front of her and presented her with a basket from behind his back. It was laden with the finest of fruits, nuts, and berries.

'Would the lady of the house kindly take a seat.' Adam inclined his head towards the mat which Eve had returned to its place. 'This morning your food has come to you.'

'And what is the occasion?'

'Does there have to be one?'

'I guess not,' she replied, tousling his hair.

Adam looked thoughtful for a moment then placed one finger under her chin and turned her face to his. He looked at her, his eyes serious. 'On the occasion of my unending love and passion for my beautiful wife,' he offered, bowing low and in the process losing a few berries which rolled along the rock and over the edge. 'Sit, my wife, and I will serve you.'

'Oh Adam, I think I'll keep you.'

'Forever?'

'And ever ... and ever,' smiled Eve. She lowered herself back onto the mat and together they shared their meal and watched as the warm rays of the sun brought the garden from its slumber.

But evil had entered paradise. It did not belong on the earth; in Eden; in the garden. It was born of discontent, distrust; an unwelcome visitor seeking out its prey.

Satan watched the man and the woman, his face hidden by leaves and branches. They were laughing and talking. He had watched them many times: bathing, eating, dancing, exploring, discovering, loving.

He had watched, unseen by the man and his wife, as they walked with the Lord God in the garden as evening fell, and as they knelt at His feet by the river, listening, learning, worshipping. And he wanted their adoration, their devotion, their love.

It was time.

He made his way down to the river and crossed to the other side. He sat under the tree and waited, motionless. He did not have to wait long. A serpent slowly wound its way along the path in front of him and mounted a large flat rock. It stretched out its long scaly body to bask in the sun. Its skin shimmered, reflecting the sun in iridescent colours of greens and pinks, and it closed its eyes to the glare.

Satan quietly pushed himself up onto his hands and knees, keeping his eyes on the serpent. He stood to his full height and approached the rock where the serpent lay, placing one foot in front of the other so as not to startle the creature. As he reached the edge of the rock, his foot scuffed some loose pebbles and he froze. But the serpent did not stir.

He slowly bent towards the creature, his eyes focussed on

its mouth, and in the blink of an eye, he entered the serpent.

The serpent's body jerked. Its eyes opened and darted around. No longer in control of its body, it slid quickly down the rock, across the ground, and up the trunk of the tree: the tree of the forbidden fruit.

The birds in the tree took flight, startled at the sudden arrival of the intruder as it settled in the fork of the tree. The serpent waited, its head protruding, watching the bank opposite.

The man and his wife finished their breakfast. There were a few coals remaining from the previous night's fire and Adam coaxed it into life and began to warm some water in the rough pan he had fashioned from a rock. It had taken him many hours to chip away at it, gradually forming a deep hollow. Although the rough pan took a while for the heat of the fire to transfer to the water or to whatever they were cooking, it also took a long time to cool, keeping the food or drink hot for quite some time. He had plans to make similar vessels in a variety of different sizes, some of them for keeping things cool as well as more for cooking.

They took their hot drinks down to the river and sat on the overhang of a rock with their feet dangling in the water. Eve had added the yellow peel of one of the tree fruits and a dash of honey to the water as it heated and the drink was sweet and tangy. Perhaps a little too tangy this time, she thought, but quite refreshing, nevertheless. She had a number of activities planned for the day and went over them in her mind, ordering them.

After tidying their sleeping quarters, she intended to take the basket with her and gather leaves. Not just any leaves – ones that smelt good. Later that evening when she had finished cooking their meal, she would heat some water then dispense small amounts of it into all the empty bowls she had accumulated, and then to each one she would add the different leaves she had gathered. Then would come the fun part.

Adam loved to taste new things: food, drink; it didn't matter. On her 'gathering walks', as she liked to think of them, Eve had not yet failed to come back with some fruit, berry, nut, herb, or seed, that they had not yet tried.

Admittedly, there were some failures amongst the successes, and Adam made no pretence when giving his opinion. 'Arrgh,' he had offered, when at first tasting the bitterness of some of the berries. 'Blech,' was another frequent response, accompanied by one of a number of facial expressions that he seemed to have perfected: various combinations of screwing his nose up, sticking his tongue out, grimacing, and frowning.

Many of the green plants Eve had served Adam had rejected after just one mouthful, and he did not hold back in his descriptions of these either, leaving her in no doubt whatsoever that one mouthful was all he intended to eat, if that. 'Tastes like grass,' was one of his favourite descriptions. 'How do you know what grass tastes like?' she would reply. 'You can't expect me to eat that,' he would sometimes say, poking at something on his plate that he did not recognise. Usually she said nothing and continued eating. She would watch him out of the corner of her eye, though, knowing that most things he would end up tasting when he thought she wasn't looking.

Once, when she had come across a low growing bush with large green pods on it, she had placed them in her basket and brought them back to try for their evening meal. Each pod had six or seven seeds inside it which she had removed, and she boiled them in some water over the fire. She had served them with a variety of other green plants.

Adam had made his way through a few mouthfuls of the more familiar greens when all of a sudden he had stopped chewing and had wrinkled his nose in disgust. He had then proceeded to put his plate aside and walk over to the fire where he unceremoniously spat.

She had looked up at him, one eyebrow raised.

'Obviously, you have not yet tried these,' he had said, pointing to the little pile of beans that remained on his plate.

She had rolled her eyes, knowing that her husband had a tendency towards the dramatic, especially when it came to eating something new. He had watched her as she picked up three of the smooth greyish beans, popped them into her mouth, and started chewing.

She had maintained a blank expression on her face for as long as she could, but had eventually lost her struggle. The beans had turned to mush in her mouth – bitter mush. She had put off swallowing them, hoping that her husband would give up scrutinising her face for a reaction so she could deposit the chewed beans into her hand and discard them in the grass beside her without him noticing. But he was attentive.

She had eventually forced herself to swallow the unpalatable mush and had then smiled triumphantly at her husband. 'Not bad,' she had said, and continued eating.

Adam had just shaken his head, adding the beans to his list of 'what not to eat under any circumstances'.

Three nights later, Eve had cooked the beans again, this time without the tough grey skins. It had taken her a long time to pick the skins off, but she had been determined.

Adam had picked one off his plate and examined it. 'This looks familiar, wife. Didn't we have something like this one another night?' He had given his wife a 'you can't fool me' look and had pushed the rest of the beans to the side in a neat little pile.

Hmmm, Eve had thought, as she chewed her mouthful of now skinless beans. Mashing might improve them ... maybe some herbs ... a little of that pungent bulb that grows down near the river, crushed and mixed in. She would not give up that easily.

As they sat by the river, Adam drew in the dirt with a long stick. He too had plans for his day. They had been quite comfortable living in their shelter. The overhang of rock provided shade and they had lined the floor of the shelter with soft bracken fern which they replaced every few days when it began to dry out. But ... there was room for improvement, and he was excited at the prospect of using the plans in his mind and his ever-increasing skills to bring this about.

He had scouted along the banks of the river over the past few days and had found a number of rocks of different shapes and sizes which he had rolled or carried along the path to their home. He intended to fit them together to form steps that would lead from the ground up to the platform of rock – their home. Although it did not in the least bother him to have to take a flying leap off the flat rock to the ground below when he awoke in the mornings, he knew that his wife would likely appreciate being able to descend more gracefully. It would make getting up a lot easier too – less of a scramble, more of a dignified ascent.

In his mind, Adam had an idea of how he would construct the steps and he scratched the rough plan of his intended construction into the surface of the dirt next to the rock. He also intended to build some platforms on which to place all their bowls, as well as the tools and cooking implements that he had made. And something needs to be built to put leftovers in, he thought. He loved the creatures that shared the garden with them but ... well, sometimes they thought they had something in storage and it just wasn't there.

They finished their drinks and left the coconut shells by the water. Hand in hand they walked along the path by the river. The path wound its way towards the tree of life; a journey that they had made many times. The tree was magnificent – by far the tallest in the garden. It seemed as if its upper branches reached into the very heavens. No matter where they were in the garden they could see it, and they would use it as a marker, returning to it from a day of exploring or of gathering.

The week before, as they had wandered along the path, they had had a diversion to their morning ritual. Hiding in amongst the reeds, Eve had discovered a nest. A duck had been sitting on the nest and, as Eve had watched, a tiny head had poked out from under her feathers.

The next morning, there were five little ducklings sitting in the nest. The mother was out looking for food and Eve had sat, fascinated, watching this miracle of new life as the tiny creatures huddled together calling for their mother. The mother duck had eventually returned with their food and five little mouths had noisily protested at having to share the tasty morsels.

They stopped at the clump of reeds to peer into the nest. It was empty. Eve straightened up, disappointed. They continued along the path.

'Quack, quack.' As Eve turned her head, a proud mother and father rounded the bend in the river, their tiny brood following close behind.

'Oh Adam, look.'

They stood still as the little family passed by. A miracle – the blessing of the Creator fulfilled.

There were other signs of new life in the garden too: nests high up in the trees, some with tiny 'chirrups' coming from them; too high for Eve to see into. Adam, on his scrambles up palm trees for coconuts, had occasionally caught a glimpse of little heads protruding above the tops of some of the nests, and they had observed conscientious parents flying back and forth with little titbits in their beaks.

There were other surprises, too. Eve had befriended the two large grey kangaroos that came down to the river to drink in the evenings. They trusted her and she loved to stroke their soft fur and have them nibble from her hand. Lately, the female had seemed preoccupied with the inside of her pouch, often sticking her head down into it, as if inspecting its contents. Eve had noticed that the pouch appeared to be growing bigger and lumps would stick out of one side and then, while she watched, the lumps would slide across the pouch to the other side. One day, she had gently slipped her fingers over the edge of the opening and looked into the pouch.

'What have you got in here?' she had said to the new mother, as two tiny black eyes blinked up at her. She had reached in and stroked the top of the baby's head.

The baby was folded up inside the pouch, its legs around its tiny ears. A very fine down covered its skin and it had the beginnings of tiny sharp black claws. The sunlight was too bright for it and it closed its eyes. 'Well, you certainly kept that a secret,' Eve had said to the proud mother as she bounded off.

The ducks floated with the current down the river and Adam and Eve watched them until they were out of sight.

They reached the tree of life and Eve sat down under its spreading branches in the shade. The sun had risen above the tops of the trees now and the air was beginning to warm.

Adam knelt down near the edge of the river by the roots of the big tree and scooped the water into his hand, drinking deeply.

As Eve sat watching her husband, something caught her eye in the tree on the opposite side of the river. Something glinted in the dappled sunlight, and she squinted, trying to make it out. She stood up and walked over to where Adam was now splashing the cool water over his face.

'What do you think that is?'

Adam wiped the water from his eyes with the back of his hand.

'In the tree over there. Look.'

He looked over to where she pointed, shading his eyes from the glare of the sun.

'Let's go and have a look,' Adam suggested.

'But that is the tree that we are not supposed to go near.'

'We weren't told we couldn't go near it. We are just not allowed to eat the fruit.'

Eve shrugged her shoulders. 'That is true, I guess.'

They stepped carefully over rocks, making their way across the river to the bank on the other side. The serpent watched, its dark eyes unblinking, its body motionless. Adam climbed the bank first and then offered his hand to his wife.

The man and the woman came closer to the tree. The serpent's eyes held the woman's gaze for a moment. She felt a twinge of uneasiness – a feeling that was strange to her – but she quickly brushed the feeling aside. Her eyes travelled up to the fruits hanging from the branches of the tree. They were ripe and full.

'It is a pity we are not allowed to eat them,' she said, looking up at Adam.

'Did God actually say, 'You shall not eat from the tree'?' Eve started at the unfamiliar voice which seemed to come from the serpent.

'Well ...' she began. She had talked to the animals before, but they had never talked back. At least, she didn't remember any of them doing so. No. They hadn't. She would remember if they did. She found her voice again, but it sounded unnaturally high. 'He said we could eat of any of the trees in the garden except this one, neither shall we touch it, or ... or we will die.' She felt flustered.

She turned to look at Adam for confirmation. He did not meet her eyes. The serpent fascinated him and he stared at it. He had not heard any of the other creatures speaking. Perhaps this creature was somehow above the other creatures in the garden, he thought. Perhaps it was blessed with some sort of special power; maybe even power that had come from eating the fruit.

'You must be mistaken,' the serpent said to Eve, his eyes never leaving her face. 'You will not die. God knows that when you eat of it your eyes will be opened and you will be like Him, knowing good and evil.' His voice sounded soothing, reassuring, and Eve began to relax a little.

There was some sense to what the creature said, she

thought. God had power; they did not. He was able to be everywhere through His Spirit; He knew everything; He saw everything; He could do anything. They could not. But … what if they could have that for themselves? she wondered. How much better could their lives be? What if they could create? What if they could go anywhere they liked at any time? If they were like God, could they live with Him in heaven? Her thoughts raced. They had seen angels in the garden before. They knew that they were made a little lower than the angels. If they were like God, would the angels worship them too? Like they worshipped God? Perhaps the serpent was right. Perhaps they were missing out on something good. If the serpent was right and the fruit would somehow make them like God, wouldn't that be a good thing? It would make them better; greater; wiser.

The woman looked again at the fruit which was hanging down within arm's reach. She could hear her heart pounding in her ears as she thought about what the serpent had said. What would it matter if she just tried a little bite? If she didn't like it she could just throw it away. If she changed her mind after she had some, she would just not have any more. Trying it to see what it was like was not exactly the same as having some with the intention of having more, surely? The Father would not even have to know. Why shouldn't they eat this fruit anyway? After all, what was it there for if they were not even allowed to eat it?

Yes, she thought. She wanted something more; something different; something new. To want something better was good, wasn't it? She hadn't realised before, but perhaps she was a little dissatisfied with their life in the garden. Yes. That was it. She was dissatisfied. It would be quite reasonable to do something about that dissatisfaction now that she realised, and if eating the fruit would satisfy her, then that is what she would have to do.

Eve reached out a hand and touched the fruit lightly with one finger and then withdrew it quickly. Nothing happened.

She looked at Adam, but he neither moved nor spoke, and he did not meet her eyes.

'See,' hissed the serpent, 'you are still alive aren't you?' It laughed an empty hollow laugh and Eve felt indignant. It was just an animal after all. She would show it that she was not afraid to pick the fruit.

She reached out her hand and closed it around a ripe juicy globe. The serpent's eyes followed her hand. She twisted and pulled and the fruit came off easily. She turned it over. It was perfect; its skin smooth and glossy. In fact, it looked much like other fruit in the garden. She brought it to her lips and bit deep into the ripe flesh, closing her eyes.

Her husband watched her face as she ate. Her eyes met his. She reached up and took some more and held it out to him. He took it and bit into it, his eyes half closed. The juice ran down his chin.

There was a noise in the bushes.

They looked up at the fork in the tree, but the serpent was gone.

Chapter Seven

Arkellus' league had been training out on the fields when they had received the news. Gilliad had stood still for several moments, his sword poised in his hand. Latorius had ranted and raved.

'A serpent! Of all the low and deceitful tricks. I suppose he thought his chances were better if he were disguised.'

'Maybe,' said Arkellus, 'but even so, the man and woman made their choice. They were not forced to take of the fruit of the tree.'

'No, perhaps not, but it was a set-up,' Latorius fumed, as he paced back and forth.

'It is likely that they would have taken the fruit eventually anyway, with or without his interference.'

Gilliad sat himself under a tree and leant against the trunk, his head in his hands. He remembered the carving that he had seen on the door of The Great Hall. He could have warned the man and woman. Perhaps he could have told them to avoid all serpents! No, he thought. It was only now that he understood the carving anyway. As he thought about the carvings, he recalled the detail of the one that followed and his heart sank.

'Have you actually seen the man and woman in the

garden since they ate the fruit from the tree?' he asked Arkellus.

'No, but I know they are still there. Nisus and Cadius were in the garden when it happened and they spoke at length about what they saw. I have just come from The Great Hall where they gave a full report to the council. They have now returned to earth and must stay there.'

Of all the celestial beings, Nisus and Cadius had spent the most time in the garden. Ministering to the man and woman was their mission, although they were not to interfere with the choices that the man and the woman made. This, Gilliad thought, was where he probably would have failed had he been given this mandate. He would have followed them everywhere, protected them from everything, and prevented anything untoward from happening to them. This disaster would not have happened if he had been with them. He would have run his sword fair through the belly of the serpent. Even better – right between the eyes! No ... his thoughts were running away with him again. He shook his head as if to clear it. No matter what he wanted to do, he would always obey the Father.

Arkellus was right, Gilliad realised. The man and woman had chosen to disobey. Nisus and Cadius were not responsible for their choices. They were. Granted, they were deceived by Satan, but in the end it was their choice to go against their consciences by eating the fruit of the tree.

'Have Nisus and Cadius spoken with the man and woman since it happened?' asked Gilliad.

'Yes and no,' replied Arkellus. 'They said that they tried to, but the man and woman just looked right through them and gave no response. It was as if they did not even know that Nisus and Cadius were there; as if they could not see or hear them.'

'What do you make of that? They could see them before, couldn't they? When we were in the garden they could see us.'

'Yes, but their disobedience has caused something

to change so that they are no longer able to see with their spiritual eyes.'

'Then they are blind?' asked Gilliad.

'From what Nisus and Cadius said, they still seem to be able to see the things of the earthly creation, but not us,' said Arkellus. So I guess it means that their physical eyes are still working. The problem seems to be that, although they still have spiritual bodies, their spiritual and physical bodies no longer work together as they should. This would explain why they are no longer aware of us. Nisus said that he went right up to the face of Adam and got no response at all.

'What's more,' he continued, 'they seem to have gone into hiding. Cadius reported that they left the tree in a hurry, and later he saw them huddled at the back of their shelter trying to make some kind of covering for their bodies with leaves. When they had finished doing that, they took themselves into the part of the garden furthest from the river where the bushes grow dense and thick and there are few paths. When Nisus and Cadius left the garden to bring the report of what they had seen to the council, they said that the man was sitting under a dense foliage of tree ferns, his face drawn and pale, and the woman was squatting down hugging her knees and rocking backwards and forwards. They were sitting apart from each other and not speaking.'

'That's not good,' said Gilliad, shaking his head. 'Not good at all.'

'What's to be done?' asked Latorius, raking his fingers through his hair. He had stopped pacing now and had sat down. 'We have to do something. Can we not fix this?'

'No. We can do nothing. The Son was at the council meeting and we asked exactly the same thing. The only hope that the man and woman have is in the grace and mercy of the Father. It is the law of the Father they have broken. It is because they lost faith in Him that they chose to disobey and go their own way. Their lack of faith caused their hearts to close and the connection that they had with His Spirit was broken.'

'So they are no longer connected to the life of the Father?' Gilliad's mind was racing as he tried to work out what this would mean for the man and woman, but Arkellus saved him the bother of further contemplation.

'No, they are not. Their hearts have now become unclean through sin and the Spirit of the Father cannot dwell in an unclean heart,' Arkellus explained. 'They only had eternal life in Him dependant on their being connected to His Spirit. Now they have lost that and their spirits have become tainted with the effects of sin. They now have a sinful nature. It is as if they are spiritually dead.'

'So by disobeying, they have chosen to go their own way?' asked Gilliad. 'That is really what it amounts to isn't it?'

'Essentially, yes. They have chosen their own way above the way of the Creator. They have put themselves at the centre of their lives instead of their Creator. That is not how they were designed. Being cut off from the life of the Father – from eternal life – can only lead to death.'

'Big mistake,' Latorius shook his head.

'You are right, my friend. Fatal.'

Gilliad had been listening intently and his face suddenly lit up. 'If sin has affected their hearts and their spirits and brought death, couldn't the Creator somehow give them new hearts, new spirits, new life, and somehow reconnect them to His Spirit? Couldn't He just let them start again?' He was pleased with his suggestion and now stood to his feet and took over the pacing where Latorius had left off.

'Like a second chance you mean?' Arkellus stroked his chin and pursed his lips. 'I don't know,' he said, eventually. 'I suppose He could. At least, I know He could. He could do anything. But it might not be quite that simple. And even if He did, what if they sinned again? Would He then have to give them new hearts and new spirits again? Would He have to keep doing this over and over every time they sinned? There is no guarantee that they have learnt their lesson. In fact, they probably haven't.'

'True,' agreed Latorius, 'and even if they were able to receive a new heart and a new spirit and they never sinned again, I guess the generations to come would be faced with the same choice. Actually, maybe we should just look forward to the new generation. Maybe they will not fall into temptation. Maybe they will remain connected to the Spirit of Life. Mankind would have the chance to start afresh.'

'I'm afraid that is not how it works. The consequences of the sin of the first man will not only affect him but all the generations to follow.'

'What?' Gilliad looked up at Arkellus. 'But why? How?'

'The Son explained this to us at the council meeting and I will try to tell you what He told us,' said Arkellus. 'You see,' he began, after taking a moment to order his thoughts, 'when Adam was created, the Father created all of mankind.'

'But how?' interrupted Gilliad. 'Even Eve was not there. We saw her being formed from Adam's rib.'

'Yes, that is when you saw her. That is true,' agreed Arkellus. 'But everything needed to form Eve, already existed in the body of Adam. You see, Adam's body was made from the elements of the earth. These elements were formed into the structure of his body. The structure was given form and function by the Lord God.'

'Yes, I follow so far,' Gilliad nodded.

'The Lord God then gave Adam spirit by blowing into Adam's nostrils. The Spirit of the Lord flowed from Adam's nostrils into his lungs then entered Adam's heart imprinting his physical heart to form his spiritual heart. Adam's spirit was formed in his heart by the breath or Spirit of the Lord God. It flowed from his spiritual heart through the rest of his body in the same way that his blood flows from his physical heart around his physical body. As his spirit flowed throughout his body it was imprinted by his physical body, and Adam's soul, including his mind, was formed in the same way as his spiritual heart was formed.'

It was a lot to take in and Arkellus paused for a moment to let their thoughts catch up before continuing. 'Let me put it this way: Adam's physical heart and his spiritual heart were both designed to bring life. The blood brings life that flows from the physical heart to the body. The spirit brings life that goes forth from the spiritual heart to the soul. The heart, you see, is the wellspring of life.'

'What complicated beings people are,' observed Latorius. 'Makes me glad I don't have a physical body too: less to understand, less to worry about, less to go wrong,' he said, patting his chest.

'Ha! Always able to find the bright side, Latorius,' laughed Arkellus. He looked at Gilliad. 'Have I lost you somewhere Gilliad?'

'I guess I understand,' said Gilliad. 'But you said that when Adam was formed Eve was there too. I still don't see how this is possible, let alone how all of mankind could be there.'

'Don't worry, I haven't quite grasped that either,' Latorius said. 'I was just hoping you would admit it first! When the Lord God blessed the man, He told him to go forth and multiply and fill the earth, but unless I have missed something, that has not yet happened. Now that I think about it, the blessing was given even before He formed the woman.'

'It was. That is true,' Arkellus agreed. 'Let me explain the way Eve was formed and that might help you to understand. You saw the Lord God take a rib from Adam form Eve from that rib.'

'Yes, and did you see Adam's face?' Latorius said. 'The Creator obviously chose the best looking rib.'

'And she has stayed by his side ever since!' added Arkellus.

Gilliad shook his head. 'I see you've been taking lessons from my friend here!'

'Yes, but he …' began Latorius.

'Anyway,' said Arkellus, cutting Latorius off, 'Adam's rib contained everything needed to form a new life. From that one rib, the Lord God was able to form Eve's physical body. The rib also contained spirit from Adam which became Eve's spirit and that spirit, when imprinted by her physical body, formed her soul. Nothing new needed to be added. Eve inherited the physical elements needed to form her body from what the Lord God had already created in Adam, and she inherited Adam's spirit.'

'That seems to make sense,' said Gilliad, slowly. 'So, if everything needed to form Eve was present in Adam when he was formed, I guess it means that Eve was present in the body of Adam from the beginning.'

'Exactly.'

'But you said that all of mankind were present in Adam. Doesn't that mean that all of mankind – all of the generations to come – had their beginnings when Adam was formed? I still don't see how that is possible.'

'Again, I will do my best to try and relate to you what the Son explained to the council,' said Arkellus.

'Slowly,' said Gilliad. 'I am still turning over in my mind all that you have said so far. I am not sure if I have room for the rest.'

Arkellus laughed. 'Slowly then, my friend. I guess the best way to think of the Creator's command to be fruitful and multiply is to look at the flowers.'

'I could do that all day,' mused Gilliad, looking around him. He loved to wander along the banks of the river. The paths were lined with exquisitely perfumed blossoms and he often stopped to smell them and examine their detail, marvelling at the design and variety. The King's garden was liberally splashed with colour. Everywhere there were flowers: tiny ones nestled in amongst the rocks and ferns, large showy ones which grew along the banks of the river, and flowers way

99

up high in the canopies of trees, some forming fruit, others designed just to please the eye and fragrance the air.

'Oh no ... we've lost him,' said Latorius.

'Are you with me, Gilliad?' Arkellus waved his hand in front of Gilliad's face.

'Sorry. You told me to look at the flowers.'

Latorius shook his head. 'Dreamer.'

Gilliad took a swipe at him but he ducked and it missed.

'As I was saying ... the flowers. They form seeds. The seeds have everything needed to form new life. The seed grows as part of the flower, then it becomes detached and falls to the ground and grows to form a new plant; a new flower.'

'That's nice,' said Latorius. 'Thanks for the lesson about flowers.'

'What have flower seeds to do with the man?' asked Gilliad. 'And the woman for that matter? Surely new people are not going to grow from seeds like the flowers do.' Well, I have heard it all now, he thought to himself. Seeds falling to the ground from the man and woman, growing in the dirt like flowers. How strange!

Arkellus laughed. 'Not exactly. Yes, they have seed and new life will come from this seed, but not in the same way as flowers. Both the man and the woman have physical seed inside them. These seeds contain all that is needed to form a new physical body, just like the seed of the flower. These two seeds come together in the womb of the woman forming the physical beginning of the next generation.'

'I see,' said Gilliad. He would need to digest this information and think on it further. He knew a little of how a new life came about, but there were some things that to him were a mystery. Perhaps, he thought, they always would be.

'What about the spirit and soul of the new life? It will not just be a physical body with no life in it, will it?' said Latorius.

'You are right. It won't. The body without the spirit would be dead,' agreed Arkellus. 'The spirit must come from somewhere to form this new life, just as Adam's spirit came from somewhere. The spirit of the new generation is formed from a seed also – a spiritual one.'

'Just one spiritual seed or two?' asked Gilliad.

'Ah. Good to see you are paying attention. One. Two physical seeds – one each from the man and the woman – but only one spiritual seed which comes from the man,' explained Arkellus. 'You see, the moment that Eve came into being, she already had many physical seeds within her and they have been designed to mature gradually over time, but they do not contain spirit. Likewise, if she gives birth to a female child, by the time this child is born, the child will already have all the seed that she will ever produce, waiting in a state of dormancy inside her. Once the female child's seed has been formed while she is still in the womb, it becomes detached and it no longer has contact with the blood. This means it does not contain spirit. The man, however, is continually producing physical seed and, while this seed is being formed, it is in contact with the man's spirit which flows along the same pathway as the blood. This is the spiritual seed that is passed on when a new life is formed.'

'So ... the next generation will inherit spirit from Adam, but not from Eve?'

'Yes. In the form of a spiritual seed. And so the process will continue down through the generations. Each generation will be formed by physical seed from both parents but the spirit will be passed down only through the father.'

'So when the Lord blessed Adam and told him to go forth and multiply, He was actually calling forth the generations from the beginning,' mused Latorius. 'Everything needed, both physical and spiritual for all generations to come, was present in Adam.'

'Well put, Latorius,' Arkellus nodded.

'So the next generation will be like Adam then?' Gilliad asked.

'Yes and no. They will be like him as he is now.'

'You mean each new generation of husbands will sit under tree ferns, pale and drawn, not speaking to their wives?' said Latorius.

'Probably,' Arkellus said, laughing. 'No. What I mean is that, instead of being connected to the Holy Spirit – the Spirit of the Creator – through clean open hearts, they will be born spiritually disconnected from their heavenly Father, just like Adam is now.'

'What?' Gilliad was aghast. 'So because Adam sinned, it affects all the generations to follow?'

'Yes. In Adam, all have sinned. All of mankind – all the generations to come – were present, both physically and spiritually, when Adam was formed; therefore, when he sinned, all of mankind lost their spiritual connection to the Creator. Each generation will now be born into the world with a spirit that is disconnected from the only source of eternal life. Instead of being continually renewed and refreshed by the Holy Spirit – the Spirit of the Father – through their hearts, their spirits will just recirculate through their sinful hearts. They will now be born with a sinful nature. I guess you could say that they will inherit a spiritual birth defect: one that was caused by sin entering the heart of man.'

'Adam's legacy,' mused Gilliad.

'That's one way of putting it, I guess.'

'I see now why you said that there is nothing we can do.'

'Nothing,' said Arkellus. 'These things were put in place since before the dawn of creation. From eternity. Besides, matters of life and death are not in our hands. They are in the hands of the Author of Life.'

'Was the Son angry about what the man and the woman had done?' asked Gilliad. He remembered clearly the rebellion of angels and archangels. The Son had flung them out of heaven, and Gilliad suddenly felt protective of the man and the woman in the garden.

'The Son was not angry, no. There was only sadness in His eyes.'

Gilliad and Latorius had watched the Son in the garden. They had seen the great love that the Son had for the man and woman – the love of the Father revealed through the Son.

'But,' Arkellus continued, 'He did speak words of hope: words of comfort. 'There is a way' was the last thing He said before we left The Great Hall. I don't know what He meant by that, but we will just have to trust Him.'

There was nothing more to be said. Gilliad left Arkellus and Latorius in the field under the tree. He would not be able to focus on training anyway. His thoughts were miles away; down on the earth, in fact. If he stayed and clashed swords against Latorius now, he thought, he would be at a distinct disadvantage, and he was developing quite a reputation. Best not to spoil it now.

'Dreamer indeed,' he muttered, looking back at his friend. 'Oomph!'

He picked himself up. Well ... perhaps just a little. Although, he was sure that shrub was not there before ... or was it?

Chapter Eight

$\mathfrak{T}$he Son came down to the garden in the cool of the evening and He called to the man and his wife.

The Son waited and, eventually, they came. The man blamed the woman, the woman blamed the serpent, but their faces betrayed their guilt and grief. Trembling, they fell to their knees and confessed. And there, deep in the heart of the garden, they sought mercy and forgiveness. The Son reached down and gently lifted them up, and He led them down the path to the river: the path to the tree of life.

The entire host of heaven had been summoned to appear in the garden; the rebels also. The air was thick, stifling, and Gilliad could smell the enemy – sulphurous, stale, decaying. He stood with his hand on his sword, waiting, alert for signs of unrest; ready to fight; ready to defend. But there were none. The enemy milled around in silent groups.

There was movement to the right of him.

Wearing loincloths of fig leaves, their heads downcast, the man and the woman, with Nisus and Cadius on either side, were led by the Son to the tree by the river. The faces of the man and woman were pale and drawn. The woman's hair hung limp and knotted down her back. Their lips were parched, for they had not been back to the river since early that morning.

The angels and the rebels had been permitted to materialise, and the man and women looked around at the witnesses with frightened swollen eyes.

Suddenly, the blast of a horn cut the air and the Creator – the Judge of heaven and earth – descended in a pillar of flames. Then there was silence again.

The court was in session.

A scuffle broke out to the right of Gilliad and he watched as the deceiver was dragged by Michael and Gabriel through the assembled witnesses. He struggled and cursed, but he was no match for their powerful build and strength. They reached the edge of the clearing and pushed him forward. He fell, landing heavily in the dirt at the feet of the Judge.

'Rise, Lucifer, fallen one,' the Judge commanded.

He picked himself up, but he did not meet the eyes of the Judge.

'You were once an anointed guardian cherub on My holy mountain; perfect in beauty and full of wisdom until unrighteousness was found in you. Your heart became proud because of your beauty, and you corrupted your wisdom for the sake of your splendour. You tried to make for yourself a name, and in your heart you desired to be like the Most High. An eternal curse be upon you. Your time is short, for from the woman will come a Seed, and by this Seed you will be defeated, your works destroyed.'

And the deceiver was dragged from the presence of the Most High God.

The Judge now motioned the woman to step forward.

The Son gently placed a hand on her shoulder. 'Go,' He said quietly.

She took two unsteady steps and then fell to the ground, her face in her hands. Her cries carried on the air through the quietness of the garden – heart-wrenching, shuddering sobs; cries of remorse, of painful regret; cries for mercy.

'Rise Eve, mother of all living,' said the Judge.

She slowly rose to her feet, her legs weak from anguish, her face drained of colour. She wiped her tears away with dirty hands. She could not look into the eyes of the Father, and her head hung down.

The Father spoke gently. 'Eve, because you disobeyed Me and took of the fruit, your blessing will be cursed. This curse will be for you and for all generations to come; for in pain and with sorrow shall you bring forth children. And because you gave the fruit to your husband, he shall rule over you.'

The woman stood sobbing quietly now, her arms hanging limply by her sides.

The Judge turned to the man.

'Adam, man taken from the red earth.'

Adam stepped forward to join his wife, his head hung low, his eyes were downcast. He swallowed hard, struggling to maintain his composure, then he dropped to his knees in the dirt at the feet of the Judge. His shoulders began heaving and he clasped his hands tightly together against his chest as his breath came in painful laboured gasps.

'Rise, Adam,' the Judge said. 'I am the Father of your spirit. I gave you life – eternal life. But because you have sinned against Me and eaten from the tree, you are now cut off from that life. Through you, all generations to come will be born under the curse of death – the payment for sin.

'Because of your sin,' the Judge continued, 'I will also curse the blessing that I have bestowed upon the earth, whose abundance has sustained your body. You are now destined to spend the remainder of your life in toil. By the sweat of your brow you will struggle to bring forth food from the ground, for it will yield thorns and thistles.'

The Judge now addressed both the man and the woman.

'No longer will you live in the garden that I planted for you; neither will you be allowed to reach out and take from the tree of life, for sinful man must not live forever on the earth. Man was made from the dust of the earth, and to dust he will return at the end of his days.'

As Gilliad watched, the roots of the tree withdrew from the river, its sustaining gift no longer flowing into the waters that ran through the garden, through Eden; no longer giving its gift of life to the waters of the earth.

The sentencing was over; the court no longer in session.

The angels parted as the man and the woman were led by the Son along the path next to the river; led to the edge of the garden. And there they crossed the threshold into the unknown.

And at the east gate, the Lord God placed cherubim with flaming swords to guard the way to the tree of life; for man had chosen the way of death.

Thwack.

Dark red blood spurted from the neck where the head was severed. The head rolled over the edge of the rock – the altar. An innocent victim the sacrifice. The blood pulsed from the fatal wound until the heart stopped beating. One life given for another. It oozed down the rock face, slowing to a trickle as it reached the ground – a bright red stain – a blemish on the face of a perfect creation.

Bile rose in Adam's throat and he looked away as he fought waves of nausea.

Eve stood some distance away from her husband. She watched the slaughter in silence, her hand raised to her mouth, pressing against her trembling lips, her vision blurred by the tears streaming down her face, leaving tracks in the smears of dirt on her flushed cheeks.

The Son stood by the rock, His sword raised, its sharp

edge stained with the blood of innocence. He had called the animal to Him in the garden and it had come. He had led the man and the woman from the garden carrying the animal on His shoulders, and when they had reached the rock, He had lifted it from His shoulders and gently placed it down. And with trusting eyes it had watched the face of the Son as He laid it on the altar.

The Son made garments of skin for the man and the woman to cover their nakedness; to cover their shame: shame birthed from guilt; guilt from sin.

Then the Son left.

And the man and the woman were alone.

The rebels had fled, fear in their eyes, but those who trusted, those who were faithful, had remained in the garden. In the blink of an eye, they had been returned to heaven, to the King's garden, where sinful man cannot dwell with a holy God.

The battle of good and evil had begun. The stakes were high: the heart of man.

An urgent council meeting had been called, and Gilliad and Latorius waited outside the doors of The Great Hall. There were many others, milling around in small groups of twos and threes. Gilliad walked over to the closest entrance and cupped his ear against the door.

Latorius smiled and shook his head. 'A bit too thick, my friend!'

Gilliad's frowned.

'Not you ... the door!'

'Humph,' snorted Gilliad.

They found a bench and sat down, but Gilliad was restless.

'Go down to the river. Eat something,' Latorius suggested. 'Sit there for a while. I don't think they will be coming out anytime soon.'

Gilliad stood up and took a few steps down the short path that led between garden beds towards the street and then stopped and looked back.

'I can come and can get you when they do,' said Latorius.

His friend was right. There was nothing he could do, so he may as well fill in the time down by the river. He made his way along the wide paved golden street that led past The Great Hall. He veered off the street onto a narrow path which meandered through vine-covered arbours down to the river. Not to his favourite spot, though. That was too far away, and if there were any developments he wanted to know immediately.

He thought he would not be able to eat, but once there, he realised that he was ravenous. He picked an armful of fruits, nuts, and berries and then settled down under a tree, one eye on The Great Hall. Not much could put him off his food he realised. Probably nothing, now that he came to think of it.

He ate until he had had his fill, and then knelt down and scooped water into his hand. While he was still leaning over the river the horn sounded, and he looked up to see Latorius running down the path towards him. The great doors had opened and the archangels were just beginning to spill out of the openings in search of their charges. A general assembly had been called.

They spoke in low voices. The mood was subdued. The joviality that accompanied most of their gatherings was absent, as, notably, was the food. It was just as well he had already eaten, Gilliad thought. They might be here for a while.

Finally, all of the angels had taken their places at the tables around the tiers of The Great Hall; all except two: Nisus and Cadius. 'Above all, never leave your charges,' they had been told. They would be informed, in due course, of the proceedings of the meeting.

The Son had spoken to the archangels at the council meeting, and now Gabriel would preside over the assembly, conveying to the gathering the essence of what had been discussed. The assembly rose as he mounted the steps to the platform. He turned to face the expectant gathering and then motioned for them to be seated.

He waited for a moment until the scraping of chairs had subsided.

'On this day you have become warriors,' he began, 'fighters on the side of good, defenders of the truth. Be assured, your training has been thorough and you have proven that your hearts are loyal. You are well-equipped to fulfil the assignments that the Father has prepared in advance for you to do.'

There was a murmur of agreement throughout the hall.

'You will not actively engage the enemy in warfare except to defend those in your care. Vengeance belongs to the Lord and it is His to repay.'

At this, Gilliad noticed disappointment on the faces of some of those around him. Some of them, he was aware, had discussed the possibility of a direct attack on the rebels, but he knew that they would not act on their own emotions, their own judgement. They would obey the Father.

Gabriel, it seemed, was aware of this sentiment. 'The enemy will not go unpunished,' he assured them. 'As you no doubt are aware,' he continued, 'most of your assignments will take place on the earth. These assignments will vary, depending on the gifts the Father has bestowed upon you. Between assignments you will return to heaven for training and for a time of refreshing in the house of the Father. Each league will be assigned an area. Each area will be under the guidance and authority of an archangel – the leader of your league.'

Good, thought Gilliad. He had confidence in Arkellus

and he had no qualms in doing whatever his leader asked of him. There was an unspoken trust between the leader and those under him and Gilliad had never felt the need to question any of his decisions.

'What I have to say to you now may seem as if it relates to a time a long way off, but I assure you, before long, the earth will be filled. Mankind will soon begin to spread throughout the earth. From the first man and woman will come numerous offspring. Their offspring will give birth to many children, as will their children and their children's children.

'Each time a child is brought into the world, one of you from the league responsible for that area will be assigned as the child's guardian. This may be for a time; it may be for the entirety of the child's life. That will depend on the child. For when the child knows enough to choose the good and reject the evil, if he or she turns away from the Father – if they choose to go their own way – the child's heart will close and your assignment will be suspended, for the child will no longer be under the grace of God. However, should the child's heart remain open through faith, then he or she will remain under the grace of God, and you will continue to minister to him or her.

'You will also be assigned to minister to and protect those whose hearts, through faith, have re-opened to the Lord, for they will again come under the Father's grace. There will be times when you may be required to form a hedge around those in your care to protect them from the rebels, and you will need to call upon others in your area to help. Those of you who are not assigned as guardians at that time will need to be ready to come to the aid of those who are guardians. There will be times, however, when you must step back. You cannot interfere with the choices of mankind. They will be living in a fallen world and they cannot avoid the consequences of sin, including death. In your heart you will know what is required of you.'

It was a lot to take in and Gilliad listened intently.

Already, he had many questions forming in his mind.

'Should those who are in your care move to another place on the earth, you must leave your area and remain with them, only returning to your area to be reassigned when your charge's life in the body is over or they no longer come under the grace of the Father. If for any reason your charge must be left, you must first call on a substitute to step in during your absence.

'If children in your care die, you will escort them to a place which the Father has set aside within the walls of heaven. It lies beyond the King's garden. Some of you will be assigned to care for these little ones: to bring them up under the watchful eye of the Father.'

Well, that took care of one question, thought Gilliad. He looked sideways at his friend and smiled to himself. Latorius was sitting on the edge of his seat, concentrating intently on what Gabriel was saying. Just the sort of assignment that would suit him too, he thought. After a while though, he would probably yearn for some of the action down on the earth. By now, he knew the nature of his friend almost as well as he knew himself.

His mind wandered as he thought about the place for children. Gilliad recalled the vast areas of land that he had seen beyond the garden as he trained in the expanse above. He had always intended to explore further, but now he would have a good reason to do this. Somewhere within the walls of heaven, there would soon be children laughing and playing, delighting in the beauty around them and in the goodness of the Father's provision, and he found himself looking forward to sharing his home with these little ones.

He thought of the things that he would like to show them: the honey bees in the trees, the nests of eggs that lay hidden amongst the reeds by the water, his favourite fruits. He imagined hoisting them up onto his shoulders and soaring through the air above the treetops, listening to their squeals of laughter as they clung on tight while he turned somersaults

113

mid-air, and as they felt the wind rushing past their ears.

But his thoughts were running away. Again. 'Focus', he whispered, causing Latorius to glance sideways at him and raise an eyebrow. He brought his attention back to what Gabriel was saying. Still talking about the children, he realised with relief.

'... the close of this assembly, work will commence on their home in heaven – the paradise for children – and some of you will be assigned to this task. The Master Architect's plans were unveiled in the council meeting and, as with all of His designs, both in heaven and on the earth below, they are very good.'

'The paradise for children,' whispered Latorius, attracting a return glance from Gilliad. Well, he thought, if I cannot be permanently on assignment there, it will certainly be a frequent mid-flight stopover, even if I have to detour. He looked at Gilliad again and raised both his eyebrows this time, unspoken words passing between them. Gilliad just smiled and shook his head.

'The children will know that they are loved and cherished and they will not be lacking in any good thing,' assured Gabriel, quite unnecessarily. 'They will live in beautiful homes. There will be many areas in which to play, trees to climb, animals to care for, birds to feed, places to explore, and much for them to learn. Many of these children will have passed from the womb straight into heaven and they will know nothing of the things of the earth. You must teach them, for someday they will return. You must tell them of those they have left behind on the earth; those who grieve for them. All of them will know the love of the Father in all its fullness, for all are His children, His family.

'As you no doubt have realised, I have only spoken about the destiny of the children: those who die before they know enough to choose the right and reject the wrong. The Father does not hold these little ones accountable and they will not be subject to judgement.'

Gilliad nodded. Another question answered. It was in the nature of the Father to be gracious and merciful. He knew that. In fact, he would have been surprised if it were otherwise.

'You will be aware that because of sin mankind has been cut off from the Spirit of the Father,' Gabriel continued. 'Mankind cannot remain on the earth in a sinful state. That is why they now have a limited lifespan. Their bodies will one day return to dust. But they cannot live with the Father in heaven, for sinful man cannot dwell with a holy God. There has to be a place for man to go once he departs his body, for his spiritual body – his spirit and soul – will endure. When man takes his final breath and his heart ceases to beat, his spirit and soul will depart his body. His spirit – the life of his soul – will return to God who gave it ...'

Good, thought Gilliad with a sigh of relief. I must have misunderstood after all.

'... and his soul will depart to the abode of the dead within the earth.'

What? Gilliad sat upright. Of course. Now he remembered. The spirit is the gift of life and can be divided from the soul. But all souls to depart to the abode of the dead? How could a loving God do that? Gilliad wondered. It hardly seems fair, he thought, to treat the righteous in the same way as the unrighteous. He saw on the faces of those around him that others seemed to be thinking the same thing. Surely those who had been in their care – the faithful – would not be going to the lake of fire. But he was not aware of any other place below the earth's surface. Arkellus had spoken of the lake of fire after Lucifer had rebelled and incited others to follow.

'Although the souls of the righteous and the unrighteous – the faithful and the unfaithful – will both depart to the abode of the dead, there are places being prepared for each. These places will be separated by a wide chasm that no one can cross over. When the souls of the unrighteous depart their bodies, they will continue down past the abode of the righteous to the abode of the unrighteous deep within the earth where there is darkness. Here there will be sorrow and mourning. There will be no rest; no peace. Within this abode there are also dungeons of deepest darkness held in reserve for those who have allowed their sinful hearts to sink to the darkest depths of evil.

'The unrighteous will remain in this place until the Day of Judgement. It is from the depths of this abode that a shaft leads down to the lake of fire prepared for the devil and his angels. The lake of fire will also be the final destiny of the unrighteous: those who, whilst in the body, continued to reject God's love and mercy.'

The assembly was silent, each one contemplating the grim words of the archangel Gabriel. The price of sin was high – eternal death – separation forever from the life of the Father, and there was a finality about what Gabriel had said. Gilliad shuddered.

But Gabriel now spoke words of hope. 'When the faithful in your care depart their bodies and their spirits return to God in heaven, you will escort their souls to the abode of the righteous just below the surface of the earth. In the abode of the righteous, there will be comfort and peace – a paradise of sorts within the earth – a shadow of the garden that was lost. They will remain under the grace of the Father, for His eyes are always on the righteous. Some of you will be assigned to care for these faithful ones until their salvation; until the curse of death is broken by the Seed of the woman. For then the Father will raise them up and they will again see the light of day.'

And Gilliad remembered the words of the Son: words of hope, words of comfort. 'There is a way,' He had said.

This way, the only way back to eternal life then, was the Seed of the woman: the Saviour promised to mankind; the One who would defeat the works of the devil and reverse the curse of death.

Then faith in the Seed of the woman was really the only

hope for mankind, Gilliad realised; faith in the Seed of the woman was the only hope for the restoration of what had been lost because of sin; the only hope for eternal life.

And suddenly it became clear to him: This message of hope must be preserved and passed on to all generations to come. The message was greater than the mission.

No … the message *was* the mission.

Part Three

Chapter Nine

Gilliad sat down on the closest stone bench to gain his bearings. Whenever he returned from an assignment, he was struck by the intensity of the colours and the purity of the light, and it took a few moments for his eyes to adjust.

The colours on the earth had dulled since the curse. It was a gradual dulling. If he had nothing to compare it to, he probably would not have noticed. It was only when he returned or when he was reassigned to the earth after a period of leave that he noticed the marked contrast.

His eyes quickly became accustomed to the change, but he remained on the bench watching the gate as guardians came and went. He liked to think of this pathway that linked heaven to earth as a staircase of sorts – a very busy one at that.

He was about to get up when, suddenly, one of the guardians burst through the gate with a holler and broke into a forward roll before landing on his feet and punching the air. Latorius ... of course! Who else would make an entrance like that? thought Gilliad, shaking his head.

He watched as his friend took in his surroundings, squinting first through one eye then through the other, his hand failing to shade his eyes from the brightness. The absence of shadow was another thing that took some adjusting to, for, unlike the earth, there was no sun, no moon. The light was even. It did not seem to originate from a particular point. It was just there ... like the air.

Latorius opened both eyes, and Gilliad began to walk towards his friend.

'Gilliad?' Latorius broke into a run of sorts, dodging a fountain, leaping over a bench, and almost colliding with two archangels who were deep in conversation on their way to the sanctuary.

'Whoops! Sorry, pardon me, apologies ...' he managed to blurt out as he spun around them.

He grabbed his friend by the shoulders, panting and laughing at the same time. 'You've just arrived too, then?'

'That is what I seem to have done,' agreed Gilliad. They had rarely managed to have leave at the same time. If they met at all in heaven, usually one of them was about to finish their leave and the other had just arrived.

'What on earth have you been doing to get a grip like that?' Gilliad rubbed his shoulders where two large handprints remained.

'Holding back the enemy of course! What else would I be doing?' Latorius grinned.

'Come, sit down. I think you must need longer than I did for your eyes to adjust,' said Gilliad, looking pointedly in the direction of the backs of the retreating archangels.

'Humph! They should look where they are going.'

They had seen very little of each other whilst on deployment. The area to which they had been sent was the tiny land known as Judea. This was the area in which most of their assignments had been, or at least where most of them had begun.

Under instruction from the Father, Gabriel had deployed many leagues to this and the surrounding areas, for it was the land the Father had given to His chosen people – the Israelites.

The Roman Empire now governed the tiny province of Judea, and relations between the Romans and the Jewish people were generally civil. The country had, several hundred years before this, been ruled by the Greeks, and with them they had brought the worship of pagan gods as well as many religious ideas from Greece and the Orient. Buildings, monuments, statues, and temples to false gods abounded, and astrology and magical practices were rife. The Roman Empire had largely continued these practices, although, under Roman rule, the Jewish people were permitted to practice their religion and worship in their synagogues.

Gilliad and Latorius had been appointed as guardians of children – one Roman, one Jewish. They had both been largely stationed in Jerusalem, the capital of Judea, and the children had lived for a time in bordering neighbourhoods. On occasion, the children had both been with their mothers at the markets at the same time, but that was about the extent of the possibility of the guardians' paths crossing.

The family of the boy for whom Latorius had been guardian were nominal Jews; at least that is how Latorius saw them. They went through the rituals, they visited the synagogue, they observed the Sabbath and the celebrations and feasts as was required of them under Jewish law, but behind closed doors, their lives did not reflect faith in the God of their forefathers.

The young boy, however, had recently shown quite an interest in the matters of the heart. He had taken to dropping into the synagogue after his daily lessons, which were attended to by a strict and well-respected Jewish scholar whom his father had known since his own childhood. In the synagogue he would often sit for hours at the feet of the Rabbi to listen to the words of the Torah.

He was a bright child and had memorised the words of the Shema, a statement of Jewish beliefs, and the Hallel, part of the Book of Psalms, and his teacher was beginning to take him through parts of the Book of Leviticus. He would lie in his bed at night thinking over these words and pondering them in his heart, and in the quietness of his room, he would kneel on the hard floor beside his sleeping mat and talk to the Father. Just like Daniel had. One of the Rabbis had told him the story of Daniel. He wanted to be like Daniel – to be brave and strong; to stand up for what he believed in no matter what. He couldn't understand his mother and father. They said they had faith, but, for the most part, they didn't act like they did.

When the boy was an infant, Latorius had spent a few years in Bethany, close to the capital. The family had gone to stay with the boy's maternal grandparents for a time. They were a poor family, and the father, who was a tentmaker by trade, had struggled to find work in Jerusalem. They had eventually returned to Jerusalem, however, and had leased a small plot of land on the outskirts of the city from the brother of the boy's mother, where they had grown small crops of beans and corn to sell at the markets. The mother of the boy also earned a small income by sewing and mending clothes for some of their more wealthy neighbours.

They lived close to the city boundary in a tiny two-room house. Much of their income went into the pockets of the landlord. They kept a goat and a few fowl and, although food was far from plentiful and they rarely ate meat or had enough milk or cream leftover to make butter or cheese, it was enough. There were three children now – two girls and a boy – and another on the way. They had clothes, they had sandals, and they had a roof over their heads. Money was tight, but they managed.

Latorius had grown fond of the boy. He had been reluctant to hand over his charge to another guardian, but he knew that he would be leaving the boy in good hands. Usually he was permitted to remain on assignment with his charge for as long as they remained under the grace of God, but Arkellus had told him that he was to be reassigned.

Gilliad had started his assignment in Jerusalem a number

of years before Latorius when his charge was born, but the family had, of recent times, settled in Galilee. The father of the boy who he had been guardian for was a painter, but like the tentmaker, there was not enough work. There were many painters in Jerusalem, and he had eventually decided to pack up his family and move north to look for work. There was a limit to the extent to which one could undercut the prices charged by other businesses, and he had reached it.

They had stopped at a number of places on the way to Galilee: Lydia, Samaria, Nazareth, and Cana, but always he had found the same problem – not enough work. Eventually, he had stopped in the small fishing village of Magdala, by the Sea of Galilee.

He had started small, going down each day to the shores to seek out work. He would strike up a conversation with the local fishermen, many of whom he had noticed had boats that were in need of a coat of paint. He would ask them about their catch that morning, give them a hand to haul it in, and help pack it into the large baskets that would take it to the markets. Eventually, he would get around to suggesting that their boats could do with a fresh coat of paint and, believe it or not, he knew just the person who could do this. He was good at what he did: good at selling his skills and good at painting, and by the time Gilliad had left his charge, the painting business had become quite profitable.

In their later years of schooling, the two boys were able to be educated at home, for their father could afford to pay for a Greek scholar to give them lessons. The teacher had taught the boys six mornings a week, and they had become quite proficient in several languages, had a good grasp of mathematics, and a fair rounding of the arts and culture, mostly Greek, of course. They had also learnt the lyre and had been expected to practise each day, although, in reality, they had usually managed to avoid this.

The younger child, the brother of Gilliad's charge who still had lessons by the scholar, loved to accompany his father down to the lake, and some mornings would venture down there by himself before anyone else in the household had risen. He loved to watch the boats coming in to the shores laden with nets full of fish, and he was often there at dawn sitting on the rocks near the shore listening to the rough talk of the fishermen as they cleaned their nets and scrubbed the cedar decks of their boats. Sometimes, they would allow him to help them.

'Give the boy a go,' one of them would say, and someone would throw him a brush and a bucket.

He would scramble on board without a moment's hesitation and scrub until his arms ached and he could no longer feel his fingers.

The fishermen would let him work alongside them and his little ears would burn at some of the language that found utterance from their lips and from the stories that they told while he was working, but he was careful not to repeat what he heard at home, for he knew that his mother would likely use the rod on him.

When the work on the deck was over, suddenly the fishermen would appear to remember that he was there. 'Throw the lad a fish,' one would say. And someone would reach into a basket of flapping fins and tails and extract a large musht. Just one of these fish would be enough for each member of his family to have a substantial portion, and although his mother scolded him if he spent too much time down by the lake, she was always secretly pleased when he came back with the makings of their main meal.

They usually ate twice a day. The first meal of the day was the heartiest. The boys' mother would rise before dawn and prepare a fire in the hearth behind the house. She would knead some dough made out of either wheat or barley flour, and it would be left to rise on a heated stone plate, then kneaded again and formed into a thin circular cake and cooked in a shallow clay pot in the oven.

If the younger boy came back with a fish, she would place it in a lidded clay vessel with some olives, herbs, and leeks, and cook it alongside the bread. She would always get the boy to clean the fish, though. The father would return from the lake to join his family for the meal, and together they would eat the bread and the fish, both drizzled with olive oil. Sometimes, the fish it would be sprinkled with almonds or pistachios if they had them. Most of the time they didn't.

The boys' father usually took a small parcel of food wrapped in a cloth with him to eat during the day as he painted down by the lake. His wife would also wrap up a parcel of raisins, nuts, leftover bread, and some fruit: usually a few figs or pomegranates; sometimes a small bunch of grapes. Oftentimes, after the boys had finished their lessons for the day, their mother would send them down to the lake with some milk or cheese for their father, and they would sit there with him while he ate, hoping to attract some small morsel for themselves.

'You boys haven't been working hard enough to deserve this,' he would say, as he pulled off a chunk of bread and popped it in his mouth. But he would usually give them some anyway.

In the evenings, when the boys' father returned from the lake, there was a simple meal such as bread and pottage: a soup made of red lentils, seasoned with garlic and oil in which a number of herbs had been steeped. His wife would have made this soup in the morning after all the household chores were completed and she had returned from the markets. The aroma would waft through the house and the boys' stomachs would growl in protest at having to wait until the evening. Sometimes, she let them eat a little food during the day: mostly fruit, or, if they were lucky, a small wedge of cheese.

'That's all you get. Now run along,' she would say, her hands on her hips.

The years had passed, and the boy for whom Gilliad had been guardian had grown. He was now a young man. He had chosen to turn away from the one true God and his heart had closed.

Gilliad's assignment had ended.

It was sad this closing of the heart, Gilliad often thought. Whenever this happened to one of his charges, his heart ached for them; ached for the innocence lost; ached for what could have been. He could not understand why anyone would choose to ignore the grace and mercy of the Father; how they could block out the knowledge of Him who made the earth and all that dwelt upon it; Him who made the moon and the stars, the sun, the sky. How could anyone ignore the witness of creation; the declaration of the heavens?

The knowledge of God and the knowledge of eternity was written in the hearts of mankind. How could they not feel accountable to their Creator? he wondered. How could they not seek Him? He just did not understand this turning away.

Although his parents 'had no time for religion', as his father would often say, the young man, as he had now become, had a curious nature, and even in his youth he had begun to dabble in the practices of the false religions around him. The Greek tutor, who had educated the boys, had filled his head with grand ideas about gods and goddesses, myths and legends, and had taken him to one of the temples in Magdala where he had watched the rituals performed by the priests and he had listened to Greek philosophers expounding their ideas.

Gilliad knew he would now be vulnerable to demonic possession. He had seen this happen before. Though a person's heart had closed to the one true God, their heart might open again through faith in a false religion or belief, and demons could then enter the person. The rebels were opportunistic. They liked nothing better than to take over the body of a person. It was then that they could do the most damage. He had seen lives torn apart by the indwelling presence of a demon, or even a number of demons.

The victims would often hear voices and their behaviour

would become erratic. Sometimes the demon would speak through them; sometimes it would cause them to lie on the ground and thrash about. Demons often caused their victims to harm themselves, and often the victims would have to be confined, sometimes even restrained by chains. Often they would harm others.

The families of those afflicted would take them to a physician who would try all kinds of cures, but to no avail, for it was not a physician that they needed, it was a clean heart; it was faith in the one true God.

This opportunistic tendency of the rebels was one of the reasons that children were appointed a guardian, for their open hearts must be guarded against the enemy at all costs. Gilliad had faithfully protected his charge, often having to draw his sword against the enemy, but the young man would now be on his own.

There was hope, of course. Gilliad had to remind himself of that ... often. Although the one who had been in his care might, for a time, put himself at the centre of his life or even embrace false gods, false religions, it was possible that he would eventually come to the realisation that he was a sinner; that he needed forgiveness, a clean heart. And the Lord was merciful and forgiving, and through faith, the person's heart would open and he would once again come under the grace of God.

Sometimes, if they had not already been redeployed, the angels would be reassigned to the same person they had been assigned to as a child guardian and they would suddenly be called back from heaven. It was at these times that Gilliad and Latorius could hardly contain their joy. They could only imagine the joy of the Father.

'Prepare a place for them!' They had heard the cry many times when they had been between assignments. It was a cause for great celebration in heaven when one of the lost was found.

As soon as a name was written in the book of life, they

were thought of as citizens of heaven. Immediately, plans were drawn up and dispatched to those who were responsible for construction. The citizens were not yet residents of course, but this did not stop the workers from referring to the houses they were currently working on as 'so-and-so's house'.

Gilliad and Latorius would often wander through the newest stages of the city – The New Jerusalem – when they were on leave. This heavenly city would one day be the home of the righteous – a bigger and better city by far than Jerusalem of Judea. And here, the citizens would finally live in peace. They would have no fear of enemy occupation, no fear of war, and people from all nations would join together under one King. For that was the promise God had given the people through the prophets of long ago.

There were now houses further than the eye could see, even from the top of the sanctuary steps. The designs for each home in the city were unique, tailored to suit the nature and the likes and dislikes of the individual, and the homes were fit for royalty. That was the mandate. They were for the children of the King. 'Spare nothing,' the Master Builder had said, and nothing was spared.

The materials used in the construction were of the best quality – perfectly cut and polished stone: emeralds, rubies, topaz, and amethyst, gold and rich timbers: cedar and oak. The homes were furnished with fine linens: pure white, scarlet, deep blues, and forest greens, exquisitely crafted solid timber furniture, and beautiful silverware inlaid with pearl.

The homes were spacious – mansions by comparison with anything that mankind had built. Even Solomon's palace in all its magnificence, Gilliad recalled, would pale in splendour beside the homes in this heavenly city.

Sometimes, when the angels were on leave, they would turn their hand to whichever skills were currently needed – carpentry and joinery, stonemasonry, even lending a hand with the interior decorating.

Latorius was of the opinion that he had quite a flair for matching colours, patterns, and textures. 'I think checks would look nice in this home,' he would comment, as he cast his eyes over the array of striped fabrics that Gilliad had laid out on the table in front of him.

Gilliad would just snort, roll his eyes, and carry on regardless. 'I do know what I am doing, you know,' he would often say. 'I have experience.' And he would take great delight in listing the occupations of the families in whose homes he sojourned during his many postings as guardian, as if he were qualified in each trade by association.

'My gift comes naturally,' Latorius would be quick to reply. Nine times out of ten, he managed to have the last word.

Always having the last word, Gilliad would think to himself. Nine times out of ten, Gilliad managed to have the last thought on the matter.

The homes of the righteous were set amongst manicured gardens and parkland. It was a garden city – an extension of the King's garden – and the city had steadily increased in area as the 'citizens' of heaven had increased.

The gardens of the city boasted magnificent water features all fed by the waters that flowed from the sanctuary. There were stone fountains in a myriad of designs and sizes: trickling, spraying, bubbling; small streams meandering over smooth stones and cascading into miniature waterfalls; ponds alive with brightly coloured fish which swam in and out between rocks and reeds and ducked under large lily pads.

There were arbours and paved courtyards, quiet little nooks with benches, soft moss-covered rocks to relax on, tables to picnic on, and wide open spaces to ... well, to do whatever one liked on. There were all kinds of fruit and nut trees, bushes laden with plump berries, and vines with fruit hanging down in bunches, ripe for the picking, growing amongst the ornamental plants and the abundant displays of flowers.

If only it were possible for the faithful in his charge to go straight to heaven when they departed the body, Gilliad often thought. Or even if he could at least give them a glimpse of what the Father had prepared for them. But that could not be, for when they departed their bodies, they were to be escorted immediately to the abode of the righteous within the earth. 'No exceptions!' they had been told.

A gentle melody drifted on the air from the sanctuary, breaking into their conversation. They had sat on the bench for quite some time, their favourite topic – the antics of their charges on the earth, as well as those of the little ones in the children's paradise – far from exhausted. They left the stone bench and headed towards the steps, planning, as usual, to make the children's paradise one of their first ports of call ... after the sanctuary, of course ... then perhaps the newer parts of the city ... the training fields ... oh, and The Great Hall.

'Must add that to the list,' Gilliad said, rubbing his stomach.

Latorius laughed. 'Anyone would think you hadn't eaten since the last time you were here.'

'Anyone would be correct!'

They mounted the steps to the sanctuary together: Gilliad – gentle protector, faithful servant, and Latorius – loyal and trustworthy ... servants of The Most High God.

Chapter Ten

Gilliad and Latorius left the sanctuary, their spirits refreshed. The Father's house was peaceful, welcoming, and they had stayed there for quite some time; sometimes singing, sometimes just sitting in silence, allowing the presence of the Father to wash over them, enjoying the respite from the constancy of the assignments they had just completed.

They made their way down the steps of the sanctuary, pausing to take in the view of the river, the garden, The Great Hall.

The closest door of the building was open and they walked across the paved courtyard, through the arbour that connected the courtyard to the street, and then followed the street towards The Great Hall. There was a small group of angels returning from the direction of the hall, and they stopped and greeted them.

They too were between assignments, and a few of them were almost towards the end of their time of leave. They spent a few moments catching up. Each of them had different stories to tell. Some had been guardians of children; others had ministered to the faithful who were to inherit eternal life and they had had the privilege of escorting their souls to the abode of the righteous.

A couple of them had just returned from area assignment where they had not had a charge in their care. This was not to say that their assignments were any easier. In fact, often the opposite was the case, as Gilliad could readily testify.

Prior to his guardianship of the young Roman boy, he had been on area assignment in the vicinity of the temple. The enemy had recently increased its numbers in this part of Jerusalem, for some of the learned Hebrew scholars had reasoned from the ancient words of the prophets that the time was near for the coming of the Messiah.

The enemy lay in wait outside the courtyard where they watched the comings and goings of the worshippers. They followed the expectant mothers, and they watched every baby boy who was brought to the temple to be circumcised, every young boy who passed through the temple gates. They listened to every conversation, and in their devious and evil minds they weighed every word, every circumstance. But they were none the wiser, for the One whom they sought had not yet come.

The angels Gilliad and Latorius met were heading towards the courtyard near the sanctuary. One of them was about to depart, for the mother of the baby for whom he was to be guardian was shortly to give birth.

It was an unwritten rule that on departure for an assignment, some of those in your league would gather in the courtyard to send you off. Sometimes they would sing you off; sometimes they would even escort you part of the way. It was a nice tradition, Gilliad thought. A family sort of thing to do.

As they talked, Gilliad's nostrils were greeted by a welcome aroma which carried on the breeze from the direction in which they were heading, and his mouth began to water. He nudged Latorius.

'Must be off then,' Latorius said cordially.

Paths led from the street towards each of the doors along the side of The Great Hall, and they made their way along the first one between the low-growing herbs that spilt over the edges of the well-kept garden. It was not an uncommon sight to see figures in white bending over hedges, shrubs, and flower beds. It was a labour of love, tending to the King's garden.

As they approached the open door they could hear the clink of silver and the sound of cheery voices. They poked their heads around the corner and were greeted by a welcome sight. Tables covered in white linen were decorated with large floral centrepieces, and bowls and goblets were being laid out in each place. On each table there was a large golden candlestick with seven candles in it. Several angels on each tier were walking from table to table lighting these candles and the highly-polished carved wooden chairs glowed in the flickering light and a faint smell of beeswax hung in the air. Preparations were underway for a banquet.

'Perfect timing,' Gilliad observed as he cast his eyes over the array of fine foods that was being arranged on the tables. He had missed these celebrations. Sometimes, he had managed to time his leave to coincide with a banquet, but more often than not, he would discover that he had returned just after one.

He wondered how many would be seated around the hall this time. It was hard to tell just by looking at the table settings, for whenever there was a feast, all of the places would be set regardless. It did not matter that many of them were on assignment.

Gilliad liked knowing that his comrades in heaven were thinking of him. He liked knowing that the table was set for him. At the close of each meal, those at the table would refer by name to each of those who were missing, and they would pray a blessing upon them in the Father's name. That was, after all, what family did.

Gilliad caught the eye of one of the angels as he brought pitchers of wine to the table closest to the door. 'Greetings my friend! Are we to expect an invitation any time soon?' he asked, pointedly rubbing his belly.

The angel laughed. He had had many such enquiries during the course of preparations. 'Soon,' he replied. 'Just doing the finishing touches.'

'Don't trouble yourself. We are quite happy to start now,' Gilliad offered.

'Ha, I have heard that one already. I think not.'

The angel continued with the business of setting the tables.

Latorius pulled Gilliad away from the door. 'Let's walk for a while ... build up an appetite.'

'I already have one!' Gilliad said, reluctantly stepping away from the door to follow him.

'We won't go far.'

'It's been a while.'

'Then a little longer won't hurt.'

They walked down the side of the building. It had been a long time since Gilliad had taken the time to look at the carvings on the doors. On the few occasions that he had been able to attend feasts in The Great Hall or when they had been summoned to an assembly, the doors had already been wide open, and because he could not see the carvings, which were on the outer sides of the doors facing the walls, he had not given them much thought.

The open door which they had just passed had carvings of The Creation on it as he recalled – highly intricate and beautiful – fine displays of craftsmanship that, as far as it were possible, did justice to the plants, the animals, and the first man and woman they portrayed.

They wandered along to the second door, and Gilliad stole a sideways glance at his friend as they drew level with it.

'Look out!' he shouted, throwing himself in front of his startled friend.

Latorius momentarily ducked, his arms thrown up over his head, but he quickly recovered. Gilliad had always called that door the 'falling door'. He had done that to him once before. He should have been prepared. He narrowed his eyes. 'That's one for you,' he conceded, marking an invisible tally in the air with his finger.

Gilliad knew what that meant. Whenever they were on leave together, they kept a score. It was harmless fun: a prank here and there, a trap set, a small but impossible errand that the other one was supposedly to go on. Sometimes, the others in their league would be in on it too.

They had rules though. You could only do something if it was your turn and turns could not be skipped. The winner of each round was the last one to have a turn before one of them departed on another assignment. That often meant, of course, that there would be multiple turns right at the end of their leave, even up to their final step through the gate.

Last time they had leave together, it was Latorius who won. Gilliad had thought that it was himself, but as he touched down to the earth, he had felt something flapping around the back of his legs. He had bent his head around to look at the back of his robe and found a long thin reed from the banks of the river hanging off the sash around his waist. He was not quite sure if that should be counted though, for he had not noticed the reed until he had arrived on the earth, landing directly in the birthing room of his next charge. However, as the prank had its origins in heaven, he guessed that he would have to count it. Point, Latorius.

It had certainly confused the midwife seeing a long thin reed waving about in the air then travelling briefly upwards before dropping suddenly to the floor. She had dipped her finger in water and held it up in the air frowning, then went over to the open window and glanced out. The leaves on the trees were still. Fortunately, her attentions were diverted by the screams of the woman and she seemed to have forgotten the strange goings-on by the time the baby was born. Just for good measure, Gilliad had pushed the reed under a low table with his foot, but in all the excitement of the birth, the midwife did not give the reed another thought.

Gilliad and Latorius peered closely at the carvings in front of them. On the first panel of 'the falling door' was the carving of the angels. Unlike the one on the first door, it was not a carving of their creation, but of the rebellion: a depiction of those who had chosen to follow Satan. Gilliad no longer thought of them as angels. They did not even resemble what they had once been, for the ugliness in their hearts was written on their faces, in the way they carried themselves, their whole demeanour, in fact. They belonged to the darkness: the darkness that dwelt in their hearts and would one day claim them, enfolding them in its eternal bosom.

Gilliad shuddered inwardly as he thought of the abyss: the dark pit with its sulphurous stench that rose in putrid waves from the eternal lake of fire. They were reality, but they did not belong to his reality, for he belonged to the light.

On the same door as the carving of the fall of the angels was a carving that depicted the temptation and fall of man: the serpent in the tree, the forbidden fruit. Another carving showed Adam and Eve being turned out into the world beyond the garden.

They walked to the next door. It told the story of a new beginning of sorts – an unwelcome beginning – of Adam tilling the soil, struggling to bring forth food from the cursed earth by the sweat of his brow. And so the struggle continued for those who came after; through droughts, famine, pestilence, and disease: thousands of years of toil and hardship, just to eat.

There was a carving depicting the birth of the first baby. Gilliad remembered this well. The woman had lain in the shelter of a cave on the soft bed of bracken and animal skins that her husband had hastily assembled. Neither of them knew what lay ahead, and they were scared.

Adam had paced at the entrance to the cave, restless, helpless. His wife lay writhing in agony as each fresh wave of pain overtook her exhausted body until, finally, with a bloodcurdling scream, she brought forth a child.

The child's name was Cain, and he was made in the image of the man.

Adam had knelt beside his exhausted wife clutching the defenceless little bundle of life – a small ray of happiness and joy in their life of struggle. He had gently swaddled the infant in skins and placed him in the arms of the mother, and she had held the child to her breast and comforted him; held him close to her mother heart.

The enemy had presented in great numbers around the cave that day, like vultures that circled around their prey in the desert. A great host of angels had been summoned to form a hedge around the little family, for the rebels had come intent on killing the child. The rebels had remembered the promise of the Seed of the woman, but they did not understand, for the meaning of the prophecy had been hidden from them.

Even to Gilliad, the prophecy was, in part, a mystery, yet to be revealed by the Father in the fullness of time. But he had understood enough to know that Cain was not the one of the promise, for Cain had been born of the seed of the man, born with a sinful nature – Adam's legacy: the inheritance passed down from the man. And like the man, he was disconnected from the Spirit of life: the life of the Father.

Eve had given birth to many children over the years. Some of them had remained close, some had ventured out on their own, building simple houses, tilling the soil, forming small communities. Others were nomadic – wanderers on the earth – tent dwellers, gatherers.

Adam and Eve had taught their children of the love of the Father, of the consequences of sin, and of the grace and mercy of God. They had told them stories of a time when the earth was new; a time when there was only beauty, only love; a time when the Lord God walked in the garden in the cool of the evening.

And they had passed on to their children the promise of the Messiah – the Seed of the woman – the Father's plan to send One who would rescue them from the fate to which they, because of sin, had been condemned.

Death had come to grieve the heart of the mother all too soon, for the elder brother had allowed sin to rule over his heart, and in a fit of jealous rage, Cain killed his brother, Abel.

And Abel's soul was escorted to the abode of the dead, deep within the earth. And so the gates of death had opened.

Gilliad and Latorius wandered along to the next door where a carving depicted the depths of depravity to which the occupants of the earth had sunk in such a short time. The people had all but forgotten their Creator and sin was rife. They were thieves, drunkards, and murderers. They were lovers of themselves: violent, vulgar, vile, having little regard for their fellow man. They indulged in unnatural relations with each other, even with animals, and they paid little heed to the natural created order. They were destructive and greedy, and pleasure, self-gratification, and lust darkened their empty hearts.

The enemy had tried to infiltrate and corrupt the pure line from which the Messiah would come, and demons had taken wives for themselves from among the women of the earth, for they had been captivated by their beauty, taken in by their painted facades, their gaudy adornment, and their false charms.

The demons had offspring with these human women, contaminating mankind with demon seed, and the offspring were giants – ruthless warriors, barbaric. For this abomination, the demons had been thrown into the dungeons of hell – prisoners awaiting the day of reckoning.

The next carving was reminiscent of the carving of the earth on the first door, for again the earth was covered in water. But the waters were not waters of life, but waters of destruction. The wickedness of mankind had increased to such an extent that the Lord God was grieved in His heart that He had made them and He sent a flood to destroy the earth, to wipe mankind from the earth, for all were found to be corrupt and all had forgotten their Creator ... all except one. Noah found favour in the eyes of the Lord for he was faithful and his line was pure, uncorrupted by demon seed.

Gilliad had to peer closely at the carving to see the ark, but there it was – a tiny dot on the tossing and roaring waves – a remnant – a tiny seed of life from which to begin again. The Lord made a promise to Noah never to flood the earth again, even though the heart of man was sinful from his youth. And the Lord blessed Noah and his wife, and his sons and their wives, and mankind again spread throughout the earth; the plan of the evil one again thwarted.

Across the top of the door was a rainbow – the mercy of the Father extending from the throne of heaven to the earth below. It was not carved into the wood of the door. It was a window, and the light from within The Great Hall and from the garden outside, passed through the rainbow so that an arc of colour shrouded those who passed, both in front of and behind the door.

Most of the angels had remained in heaven during the flood, for it had lasted many days and many nights. It was the last time that The Great Hall had seen almost all of the tables fully occupied.

They had returned to the earth gradually as the numbers of people on the earth steadily increased again, as the descendants of Shem, Ham, and Japheth, the sons of Noah, spread across the land.

They moved towards the next door, stepping around a stooped figure wearing a deep red sash. He was harvesting some of the fine-leafed herbs and adding them to a basket already overflowing with produce for the banquet. The smell of spices drifted through the windows and Gilliad breathed deeply through his nostrils.

'Ah … the anticipation.'

'The tower,' said Latorius, pointing to the next carving, intent on his mission to distract and delay.

'Yes, the tower. Fancy mankind thinking that they could actually build something to reach into the heavens! What arrogance! The perfect demonstration of what lies at the core of man's sinful heart: always wanting to be in control, wanting to be the biggest, the best, wanting to make a name for himself, wanting to be like God, wanting only to bring glory to himself. Sound like someone else?' Gilliad could rarely bring himself to name any of the rebels, and whenever it was unavoidable, he uttered the name with contempt.

'The people still didn't learn their lesson, did they?' Latorius observed, as they continued along the path. 'Not even after their language was confused and they were scattered over the face of the earth.'

'No. No, they didn't. They continued to live in total disregard for their Maker.'

'Not all.'

'True. Not all.'

'How about Abraham?' Latorius pointed to the first carving on 'the forefather's door', as it was known.

The Lord had chosen Abraham. He had made a covenant with Abraham promising to bless him with many descendants, and it was through the line of Abraham that the Lord promised to bring the Messiah – the Seed of the woman – the One who would defeat the work of the devil. The Lord gave to Abraham and his descendants land – the land of Canaan – a fertile land of mountains and valleys.

About two thousand years had now passed on the earth since the promise had been given to Abraham and since God's covenant with his descendants, the people of Israel. Abraham had not lived to see the day when the promised Messiah would come, but he had died in faith, holding on to the promise of redemption, of restoration, for he knew, as surely as the sun would rise each day, that one day he would look upon the face of his Redeemer and he would be brought up from his resting place, and he would again live in the land that the Lord had promised to him and his descendants.

This promise of redemption was passed down from generation to generation: a promise of hope, of salvation; salvation that would be for all people.

They had almost reached the corner of The Great Hall and were about to make their way around to the end of the building when the now familiar horn sounded and the doors opened wide.

The present eclipses a history lesson, thought Gilliad, as they turned and wasted no time in retracing their steps. Especially if it involves food.

Chapter Eleven

The angels spilled out onto the pathways and streets around The Great Hall. Gilliad and Latorius joined a group from their table as they walked along the street that led past the sanctuary. Some of them veered off the street in that direction, drawn to worship, others decided to wander through the streets where there were homes under construction, for a willing pair of hands was always welcome, and the remainder headed towards the training fields to brush up on their skills.

It had been a while since Gilliad and Latorius had embarked on any training exercises, so they followed the remaining part of the group towards the city boundary where the fields lay. There were already a number of angels assembled ready to pit their skills against each other, and they headed towards a group who were standing in a circle watching a fencing demonstration by two of the trainers.

The fencers were light and agile on their feet, considering their size. The swords that were used in fencing were lightweight and thin, and the handles of the swords had round sheaths which protected the hands of those in combat. Although they were different from the swords that the angels had by their sides while on assignment, they used these lighter swords to learn the techniques and then progressed to heavier weapons as their skill levels increased, until they were competent using those same techniques with their own swords.

After the demonstration ended, those who wished to brush up on their skills selected swords from the weaponry. Gilliad and Latorius chose the lightest weapons and headed back across the fields towards the trees that divided the training fields from the horse paddocks.

They removed their scabbards and their own swords from around their waists and leaned them up against a tree. It felt strange not to have that heaviness around the waist. Gilliad remembered when he had first put it on. It was after the rebellion and they had each selected their own swords from the weaponry: swords that would remain by their sides during all of their assignments. He rarely took his off, certainly not on the earth. That would be foolhardy. The enemy was always prowling around watching for opportunities to attack, always on the alert for the angels' defences to be down. But there was very little opportunity. Not on my shift anyway, he thought.

The enemy had little training – really only what they had received on the fields before the rebellion. Training required discipline, patience: something they lacked. Their attacks, as a result, were haphazard, and they lacked co-ordination. Their techniques relied on stealth, cunning, and there seemed to be little organisation in their ranks, little co-operation with each other.

The angels worked for the greater good, their goals being the same: to glorify God and to protect mankind. The enemy, on the other hand, operated from selfish motives. Often squabbles would break out amongst them and they would compete with each other. Theirs was a divided house, and it was this dissent, more often than not, that led to their defeat.

Gilliad and Latorius took their places on the court. They turned to face each other, their swords held upright before their faces.

'Rules first,' the trainer reminded them.

They lowered their swords. They already knew the rules,

but it was the rule that they had to listen to the rules before beginning; and rules about rules were rules after all, so they listened carefully.

The court was a long rectangle. If they stepped both feet out of the rectangle, the opponent would gain a point. One foot out was allowed, though. There were warning lines close to each rear boundary so they would be aware of being close to stepping outside the perimeter of the court.

There were lines set back two strides from each side of the centre. These 'on-guard' lines were where they would begin each round and the spot to which they were to return after each point was scored.

They were not allowed to change hands once play had started. This was not a problem though, for they were both proficient in the use of either hand.

The weapons they had chosen this time were for light thrusting only. The areas on the body which they could get points for making contact with were the neck and the torso, including the back. A strike anywhere else, including the arms, would not be counted, and touches that landed outside the target area would stop play. Only touches with the tip were counted, not the side of the blade.

Each round would last until the timer ran out or one of them reached fifteen points, whichever happened first. If the timer ran out before fifteen points had been scored, the fencer with the highest score for that round won. If the round was a draw, they would go into overtime and play for one final point to determine a winner.

They resumed their positions at the on-guard lines, holding the guards of their handles to their chins. They saluted the trainer and then each other.

If only the enemy were this polite, Gilliad thought.

'On guard!' the trainer shouted. 'Three, two, one.' He upturned the timer on the bench next to the tree.

Latorius immediately went on the offensive thrusting

his sword towards Gilliad's exposed shoulder, but Gilliad was quick, blocking the weapon with an upper sweep. While Latorius' weapon was still raised above his head, Gilliad launched a swift counter attack, returning his blade in an arc before thrusting the tip of the sword under Latorius' raised arm.

'Point Gilliad!' yelled the trainer.

They returned to their on-guard lines and the tournament continued.

They were fairly evenly matched: Gilliad's strong point being accuracy, Latorius' stamina. A small crowd had gathered to watch, and cheers went up whenever either of them scored a point.

The points quickly progressed to fourteen apiece and Gilliad briefly glanced over at the timer. It appeared to be only two-thirds of the way down. It seemed to be the longest round he had ever played. Then again, he hadn't fenced for some time. Perhaps his memory did not serve him correctly.

'Three, two, one.'

The next score was a long time coming. Latorius had now warmed up and he wasn't going to let his defences down easily. Gilliad tried to get in an attack first, but Latorius held him off, blocking his weapon and managing to deflect the blade away from his neck and torso, all the while awaiting the opportunity to launch a strike. A few times he made as if to lunge forward, and Gilliad had quickly extended his weapon towards him to hold back the attack, but Latorius was just toying with him.

Just before the last few grains of sand had fallen through the timer, Latorius saw his opportunity to attack as Gilliad briefly glanced down at the warning line. Extending his right leg forward, he lunged his body in Gilliad's direction, propelling off his left foot.

Gilliad looked up at his opponent just as the tip of Latorius' blade connected with the small hollow at the base of his neck. The unexpected jolt caused him to lose his balance and he fell backward landing heavily on the ground. But Latorius' momentum continued to propel him forward and the top of his foot connected with the underside of Gilliad's outstretched arm. He became briefly airborne before also crashing to the ground.

'Time!' yelled the trainer, as they both lay sprawled on the grass panting.

They dusted themselves off and shook hands, Gilliad conceding defeat. This time anyway, he thought. They handed their weapons to the trainer and the next two opponents took their places at the on-guard lines and bowed. And a new game began.

They walked slowly over to the horses that were grazing near the edge of the training fields. Several of them had new foals, and Gilliad approached one of the proud mothers. He extended his hand to her nostrils and she sniffed it and whinnied softly. She remembered him.

She carried on nibbling at the blades of new grass as Gilliad and Latorius admired her offspring. He was pure white: a young stallion, still a little wobbly in the legs, but he had the makings of a powerful steed.

'Well done, mother,' Gilliad whispered in the ear of the mare. 'Well done.' She nuzzled his neck with her soft nose as he bent down to stroke the foal who was rubbing up against his legs.

'We should visit the children,' he suggested. The horses and foals always made him think of the children.

Latorius laughed. 'I was wondering how long it would take you to say that.' His friend was predictable in some areas; in a nice way of course. He was solid, dependable, and reliable. You could count on him not to let you down. That was the nice thing about predictability, he thought.

He liked to think that others thought of him in the same way, although he knew that he had a reputation for spontaneity.

Nothing wrong with that, he thought. Life was meant to be enjoyed. He was prone to sudden flashes of inspiration and bursts of energy which just had to have an outlet, but like his friend, he would never let a colleague down. Never.

'Now?' asked Latorius. No time like the present, he thought.

'We should wash first,' said Gilliad. 'And change,' he added, after casting his eyes briefly over his friend. Latorius had grass stains on the back of his tunic where he had skidded across the ground several times, and smears of dirt on his arms and on one of his cheeks.

'The children wouldn't care.' Latorius returned the cursory glance and then looked down at his own dishevelled garment. 'Oh. Rough tournament that one,' he said. Somehow, he thought, Gilliad always managed to come out of training looking considerably more 'together' than he himself did.

They headed back towards the weaponry, entered the large double oak doors that led into the vast store, and greeted the angel in charge. They made their way through the long rows of swords hanging neatly on hooks along the walls. The weaponry was divided into many walled sections, each holding different kinds of swords, and a strong smell of iron greeted them whenever they entered.

The weapons were made in a large workshop behind the quarters and there the smell was even stronger. It was a pleasant sort of smell, Gilliad thought; distinctive, but pleasant.

Smells had memories. He liked the smell of the blacksmith's shop on earth because it reminded him of the weaponry near the training fields. He liked the smell of damp soil because it reminded him of the part of the Garden of Eden where the trees had grown close and the air was misty. He liked the smell of freshly cut grass on the earth because it reminded him of the horses that grazed in the paddocks in heaven.

Most of all, however, he liked the smell of food. Almost

any food ... except maybe the pungent smell of kidneys cooking. The family who lived next to his most recent charge frequently cooked offal, much to the disdain and disgust of the boy's mother, who would loudly complain whenever the smell wafted over the fence and in through their back door. This was a frequent occurrence, for the plots of land were tiny. So tiny, in fact, that to have a conversation without the neighbours potentially listening in, meant that the family had to almost speak in a whisper. The younger child was always getting scolded for raising his voice.

'Mother,' the boy would say loudly, 'I found a few coins near the tent at the marketplace.'

'Hush child, there is no need to broadcast your good fortune to all and sundry!' She was always worrying about the neighbours telling the landlord that they were doing well, for fear that he would put up the rent. Even though the painting business had picked up since they had moved to Magdala, they could ill afford an increase.

'Mother, father says he will be bringing home half a lamb tonight. He was paid well for the work he did last week.'

'Sshh. The walls have ears, you know.'

The child would look with interest at the walls and then back at his mother. She did say some odd things.

They passed through the weaponry to the rear of the building where there were quarters. They were used very little really, as at any given time, most of the angels were on assignment, and when they were on leave, for the most part anyway, they preferred to spend their time engaged in activities: gardening, training, visiting the children or the sanctuary, and construction. But there were times when they availed themselves of the quarters, especially after training when they felt the need to unwind or freshen up.

At the centre of the quarters was a large common room. It was furnished with a number of tables and chairs. The common room walls were lined with shelves on which stood large volumes of written works: poetry, historical tomes, botanical sketches, and so on. Gilliad had thumbed his way through the pages of a selection of books and found some of them to his liking.

The angels were all highly gifted, but in a variety of ways. The poets had the ability to bring words to life: words that sang to the heart of the reader, and he found their words uplifting, inspiring, sometimes soothing. The historians had painstakingly recorded the events of history in large bound volumes: records of the lives of those on the earth intertwined with the lives of the hosts of heaven. It read like a tapestry – the weaving together of the warp and the weft to make the fabric of history and, interspersed with the stories of the people, were stories of Michael, Gabriel, Arkellus, even Gilliad and Latorius, and many other heavenly hosts.

For the large part, the people who dwelt below were unaware of the presence of the angels. And that was how it had to be after the fall.

It would be different one day, thought Gilliad. And one day, the people would know just how many times they had been protected from the enemy, even from themselves.

Gilliad liked to think of the common room as the thinking angel's equivalent of the training fields. It was for the 'studious' types. Occasionally, he had sat himself down at one of the tables and listened to the various debates that were underway. Often, a number of them were in progress at any given time and the noise rivalled the clash of swords out on the fields.

Gilliad rarely joined in, though. Some of the discussions were much too philosophical for him. At least, that was his excuse. Sometimes, he thought of something witty to say, but the conversation had usually moved on by the time he had properly formed it in his mind. He usually ended up tuning out and picking up one of the puzzles from the shelves.

Many of the puzzles were highly intricate and proved

rather challenging to solve, however, so that usually ended unsatisfactorily too. No doubt made by one of the philosophical fellows, he often suspected, as he would replace yet another unsolved puzzle on the shelf.

Many of the angels were gifted artisans and had fashioned carvings and sculptures which now graced the homes of The New Jerusalem. Some of them were talented artists and there were now many beautiful works hanging on the walls of The Great Hall – sketches and paintings – as well as some smaller works on the walls of the common room.

Everyone, of course, made things for the little ones in the children's paradise.

'What are you going to do with that?' someone would ask.

'It's for the children.'

'That is beautiful; where is it going?' another would say.

'It's for the children.'

'What are you going to make now?'

'Something for the children.'

Not only did they make things for the children, they also taught the children how to make things themselves. There were boxes in the common room, boxes in the workshops, even a box in The Great Hall. Everyone called them 'useful boxes'. Whenever they made something, they would put little offcuts or scraps of materials in them, and then, when the boxes were full, they would take them to the children.

Whenever anyone was spotted arriving in the children's paradise with a useful box, they were immediately swamped.

'What's in this one?'

'Do you have any wooden blocks?'

'Is there any red fabric?'

'How about ...'

Often the whole box would be upended within minutes

amidst squeals of delight and anticipation.

Nothing was ever rejected. The children found a use for everything. Some of the older ones had become quite skilled with hand tools and had learnt to carve intricate figures from wood and marble and they also took great delight in making games and figures for the littler ones to play with.

The children often had a beautifully carved gift ready to present to their visitors – the bringers of the useful boxes – and there were quite a few precious carved figures made by little hands now sitting on the shelves in the common room and in various other rooms throughout the quarters.

At either end of the common room there were two long hallways off which were a number of separate rooms. Each of them had bunks in them on which, occasionally, someone could be found taking a quick nap; or a long one, as the case may be.

Like food, they had no real need for sleep, but occasionally they would avail themselves of the pleasantness of slumber, just because they could. There was certainly no napping while on assignment.

Gilliad and Latorius walked along one of the hallways to the end of the wing where there were rows of marble-lined shower stalls. They each grabbed a towel, a fresh robe, and a dark blue sash from the hooks on the wall opposite and headed into the cubicles to wash off the dirt and grass stains from their round of fencing.

There were a number of others also availing themselves of the chance to freshen up, and the noise of the water competed with the hearty singing that reverberated off the marble walls. The bathhouse was the perfect place for an impromptu sing-along, and Gilliad and Latorius joined the choir, adding their own voices to the watery harmony.

They left the quarters clean and refreshed and headed back through the training fields to the paddocks, each with a useful box filled to the brim under one arm.

The horses looked up at them in expectation.

They chose two chestnut mares and leapt onto their sleek backs, mounting them in one smooth motion.

'Hup! Hup!'

The horses took off in an easy cantor before picking up the pace once they reached the open road. They were on a mission. They had a delivery to make.

More importantly … there were children to visit.

Chapter Twelve

Gilliad loved babies. He loved children. He liked to think that babies and children loved him. At least the ones in heaven did; he was certain of that.

Whenever he visited the children's paradise, the children would clamber onto his knees vying for attention; demanding a story, a riddle, a joke. The children's paradise echoed with the laughter of youthful exuberance, and it was contagious. He always came away from his visits feeling refreshed, enthused. That's what children do, thought Gilliad. That's what heaven does. You have to become like a little child to enter the Father's kingdom.

A number of times his earthly assignments had finished in the children's paradise where he had left his little charges in good hands, and whenever he visited, Gilliad was keen to see how they were getting on. Sometimes, he would bring them little snippets of news about those whom they had left behind. The children were always excited when they had visitors who had news about their families, and questions would be fired in rapid succession. When they had exhausted their curiosity or their captor, they would trot off happily and play again.

But he was selective in the things that he told them, for sadness did not belong within heaven's walls, although he suspected that, no matter what news he gave them, they would take it in their stride. They were almost philosophical, always seeing the good in everything. They were always happy, these children, and to see the delight on their faces made his heart sing.

As the number of little ones had increased, so had the number of angels assigned to their care. The angels were handpicked; selected for their gentleness, their patience, their sense of humour, and each one had to go through rigorous training before being appointed to this specialised role.

In some ways it was a de-training, for in the children's paradise there was no need for swords, no need to be constantly on guard against the enemy, no need for combat, for they were safe. Usually, once they were appointed, these angels remained there unless they requested to be reassigned. That rarely happened.

Latorius still held out hopes of being on 'baby patrol' as he called it. He had had his fair share of being a child's guardian on the earth, but it wasn't the same. The children on the earth couldn't see their guardians. At least, that was generally the case. Sometimes, the guardians were allowed to materialise, but there had to be a good reason for doing this, and most of the time, Latorius couldn't come up with one.

Once, he had allowed himself to be seen in the defence of one of his charges. She had been playing with some stones while she was sitting on the ground in the market square. Her mother had left her to go and buy produce for the family. She had sat there next to the side of a tent, a picture of innocence, throwing a stone high in the air, then quickly picking one up off the ground and catching the airborne one in the same hand as it fell. She was good at it.

As she had sat and played, a group of older boys watched her from a distance. They had slowly approached where she sat, absorbed in her little game. She threw up a stone, turned her hand over, and grasped the one on the ground, but the toughest looking boy of the group, who had sidled up to her just out of her line of vision, had suddenly snatched the stone mid-air and run off with it while the other two boys grabbed the little pile that was on the ground.

The little girl had been too startled to cry out. Holding the empty little sack that the stones had been in, she stood up and dusted the dirt off her knees. She dropped the remaining stone into the sack. Her bottom lip dropped and a tear trickled slowly down her cheek.

The stones had been given to her by her mother's father. He had been a stonemason by trade – an occupation that had been passed down from generation to generation, father to son. He had allowed her to select rough stones from the offcuts in his workshop so that he could smooth the edges and polish them for her. It had taken him many hours to do, and she had often come in to watch him as he sat on the stool beside his bench. There were ten stones: all different; all beautiful to her. It was the last thing that he had made before he died.

Latorius was incensed. How dare they, he thought. They need to be taught a lesson.

He had grabbed the closest unassigned angel who was milling about the markets. 'Stay here,' he commanded.

He took off in the direction the boys had run. They had not gone far, knowing that the little girl would not be brave enough to pursue them. He had found them sitting on the ground at the back of one of the market tents, their heads together, examining their ill-gotten treasure.

He quickly looked around to make sure he was not going to be observed, and then he materialised. He had only done this a handful of times, and it always felt a little odd for his body to suddenly take on the physical. He would feel a sort of a jolt go through him, and then a kind of heaviness that was not there when he was just in his natural spiritual body. It wasn't exactly an unpleasant sensation, nevertheless, each time this happened, he was quite relieved to be able to return to just the spiritual.

'You boys!' he had said in his deepest, most commanding voice.

The boys looked up and their faces paled. He stood an easy head and shoulders above anyone they had ever seen. His shoulders were wide and his muscles rippled, even when he stood still. They started backing away, but the boy who was holding the stones tripped over the rope that secured the tent to a stake in the ground and the stones scattered in the dirt. The others used the opportunity to make a run for it.

Latorius advanced towards the boy – the leader of the little gang – as he lay sprawled on the ground. The boy began to scramble backwards, like a crab scuttling across the sand, and Latorius struggled to maintain his composure. It would not do to laugh, he chastened himself. The boy can see you.

'Stop!' he shouted.

The boy froze.

'Do they belong to you?'

The boy shook his head.

'Pick them up.'

The boy looked at him, his eyes wide.

'Now!'

The boy leapt at the little pile of stones lying in the dirt. He scraped them together, dirt and all, and scooped them into trembling hands.

'Up!'

The boy cautiously stood to his feet, keeping his eyes on the imposing figure in front of him.

'Take them to the girl.'

The boy hesitated. He had no intention of coming any closer to the giant who was blocking his way.

'Now!'

The boy's bottom lip trembled.

'I won't bite you,' Latorius said, trying to summon a

little charity towards the boy. Perhaps he had been a bit harsh. He had been a guardian for children like this once or twice. They were all bravado in front of their mates, but he knew it was just for show. When they were all alone, their courage often deserted them.

The boy edged past Latorius, almost falling into the side of the tent. Fine beads of sweat had broken out on his dirty forehead and Latorius could hear the boy's heart pounding.

Once the boy had reached the corner of the tent, he sprinted over to where the little girl was, sitting on the ground, her head in her hands. She was sobbing quietly now, the almost empty leather sack clenched tightly in her little fist.

The boy quickly dropped the collection of stones at her feet and then bolted. He ventured a quick look behind him, but the big man was nowhere in sight.

Arkellus had cautioned Latorius about this incident. 'Was that really necessary do you think?'

'Yes.'

Arkellus had raised his eyebrow at him.

Wrong answer, obviously, thought Latorius. He knew that look. His leader had directed it at him more than once.

'Well ... perhaps not,' he reluctantly conceded, after waiting what seemed to him to be sufficient time to appear to have rethought the matter. 'The child was happy again, though.' He just had to add that – the last word. He got the eyebrow again, of course. He knew that he had overstepped the boundaries, but he had a soft spot when it came to children.

When Latorius relayed the story to Gilliad, he laughed. 'Can't help yourself, can you?'

Gilliad liked to think that he himself showed a little more restraint. In his course of duty, he had rarely found it necessary to be visible to the human eye. However, he sometimes suspected that the babies who had been in his charge might somehow be able to sense that he was there.

He would often notice that a baby would suddenly laugh when he was clowning around, or he or she would become calm when he sang. Sometimes, when they smiled, it seemed like they were looking directly at him. 'You got a bit of wind?' the baby's mother would say. Wind indeed. Gilliad had other theories. It was at those times that he wondered if, deep in their spirits, there was an awareness: an awareness that faded as they became older.

The children in the children's paradise were certainly aware, thought Gilliad.

Gilliad enjoyed the trip through the countryside almost as much as he enjoyed visiting with the children. They galloped along the wide tree-lined streets that led away from the city, past the grassy fields where horses were grazing, and headed out into the open country where there were rolling hills with timbered patches dotted here and there.

A few small creeks fed by the river that flowed from under the sanctuary intersected the road where they travelled, and the horses' hooves echoed as they galloped over the timber bridges that were suspended over thick chains attached to great timber pillars at either end.

The countryside was quiet and peaceful, and Gilliad breathed deeply every so often, muttering under his breath the different scents he recognised.

'Ah, spruce.'

'What? Where's the goose?' said Latorius, looking around.

A little further along the track, 'ah, violets.'

'Violence. Why are you thinking of violence at a time like this?' said Latorius, shaking his head. 'Why can't you just enjoy the scenery and the smells?'

Occasionally, they passed others on horseback, and they raised a hand in greeting. Twice they stopped and dismounted to allow the horses to graze by the side of the road and refresh themselves from the cool water of the creeks. There were wild berries growing along the creek beds, and while the horses grazed, Gilliad and Latorius gathered some and sat down to eat.

'This one is new,' Gilliad remarked, turning one of the berries over in his hand.

'How could it be new?' laughed Latorius.

'To me, I mean.' He bit into the orange globe. 'Good. Very good.' Each time he was on leave, he found something he had never tried before.

'They have no idea what they are missing,' said Latorius.

'Who? The horses?'

'No,' Latorius laughed. 'They would be quite happy eating just grass if there was nothing else.' He had no proof of that, of course. None of the horses ever did eat just grass, for there was always someone wandering up to the fields with some fruit or vegetable in their hand. 'I mean the people on the earth.'

Gilliad, despite being a connoisseur of fine foods, had never really given this much thought. It was mostly his own mouth and stomach that concerned him.

'Think about it,' Latorius went on, warming to his subject. 'If you took, say, all the types of fruit in heaven, for instance, and lined them up against the variety of fruits on earth, the earthly fruit line would probably stretch from here to that tree over there.' He pointed to a willow growing downstream from where they were sitting. 'And the heavenly fruit line would reach further than from here to, say ...' he stood up and looked around. 'Well, I think we wouldn't be able to see the end of it.'

'You don't know that for sure,' commented Gilliad.

'Maybe not, but think about it. We are always finding a new one. So who's to know how many different ones there are?'

'The Son would know.'

It was the type of question the children were always asking the Son when he visited the children's paradise. How does a baby bird peck its way out of a shell? How does a fish breathe? How can a whole tree fit inside a tiny seed? He never answered them quickly. He always told them a story, and through the story they often figured out the answer for themselves. In fact, Gilliad had learnt about a lot of things simply by sitting with the children as the Son told them stories.

As they continued on their journey, the countryside began to change. The trees, which at the beginning of their journey had been scattered singly or in small patches, now merged into a dense forest where the tops of the trees met across the road forming a canopy above their heads.

The forest was alive with the sounds of birds, and they caught glimpses every so often of flashes of rainbow-coloured wings flitting from tree to tree. There were also tiny animals in the bushes. Rarely did they see them, but sometimes a bush would rustle as they passed as little creatures scurried around foraging for food.

The forest stretched for miles and miles and, after a while, they slackened the pace of the mares. There were numerous cleared paths throughout the forest, and occasionally they came across horses waiting by the entrance to a path while their riders were off exploring.

After continuing like this for some time, suddenly the road emerged from the dense canopy and they found themselves in an open clearing in front of a pair of very large gates.

They drew the horses to a halt at the gates and dismounted.

They unstrapped their scabbards and handed them to the gatekeeper and then led the horses under the brightly-coloured arches over the gates that displayed the sign: 'Unless you become like little children.'

That is no problem, thought Latorius, always feeling the reminder slightly unnecessary.

They entered the children's paradise and followed the sounds of laughter.

Gilliad and Latorius spent much of their visit taking the children for rides on the horses. The children rode bareback, holding on tight to the horses' manes. The little ones had to be led around, and they would sit up straight and proud, looking like kings and queens passing through the streets of their kingdom as they waved regally at their loyal subjects. Sometimes, they would sit themselves behind the little ones and race in the open fields amid squeals of laughter.

On their last visit, they had taken two of the older children up into the air above the fields. The little girl who had been placed in front of Gilliad had sat still and quiet, her fists gripping onto the mane, knuckles white, her eyes large and round, unblinking. When they touched down in the field, Gilliad had lifted her gently off the horse's back and she had wrapped her arms around his neck and clung on tightly. She had whispered in his ear 'thank you, Gilliad', barely able to make herself audible. He treasured those moments.

As he leant against the trunk of a tree watching the children play, Gilliad felt a slight tug on his robe. He looked over his shoulder at a small upturned serious face.

'Well, hello, my little friend. How goes it with you?'

'Alright.'

'What have you been up to since I was here last?'

'Things.'

'What things?'

'Just ... well ... this is for you,' the little boy managed. He had been standing with his hands behind his back and now thrust forward a small box.

'Well, what have we here?' said Gilliad, with an equally serious face. 'This is a surprise. Is it for me?'

The boy nodded solemnly.

'Come and sit down then, lad, and we will have a look.'

Every time Gilliad visited, the boy presented him with a gift. It was almost a ritual: the tug, the hands behind the back, the thrust of the little gift, and the 'surprise' on Gilliad's part.

They sat down under the tree, the boy as close to Gilliad as he could get. Gilliad started to take the lid off the box.

'Wait,' said the boy, his tiny hand resting on Gilliad's big hand. 'Guess.' This was another part of the ritual.

'A flower.'

'No.'

'A picture.'

'No.'

'A picture of a flower.'

The boy laughed. 'Keep guessing.'

'How about a bird?'

'Close,' the boy said. 'It's something to do with birds, but it's not a bird.'

'Hmm.' Gilliad scratched his head. 'Something to do with birds, but is not a bird. Is it messy and smelly?'

'Of course not!'

'Well … how about …'

But the boy could not wait. Off came the lid of the box. 'See. It's a nest. I made it myself.'

Gilliad looked into the little box. 'Ah,' he said. He carefully reached into the box and lifted out the tiny work of art. 'I like it,' he declared, and the little boys face lit up.

'Look! You can even eat these eggs,' the boy said, picking one of the eggs up between his thumb and finger. 'It's a nut.'

'Can I eat the nest?' asked Gilliad, his eyes twinkling as

he brought the whole thing up to his open mouth.

The little boy gasped. 'No!' he cried out. 'That bit's not food!'

'Don't tease the lad so.' Latorius had now joined them along with a child on his shoulders, another hanging from his neck, and one holding each hand.

'I knew he was only tricking me,' the boy said.

'I see you have found a use for some of those things that were in the last useful box,' Latorius said to the boy.

The nest was a woven conglomeration of twine, strips of cloth, and fine long strips of curled timber shavings that had been planed from some of the furniture made for the homes in the New Jerusalem.

'Have you brought another useful box?' the boy asked.

'Indeed we have. Two, in fact,' said Latorius.

The boy leapt to his feet and took off. He stopped, turned, and ran back.

'Where?' he managed.

It was Gilliad's turn to reply now. He thought for a moment, his face serious. 'Let's see ... left at the large fountain, straight along the path until you come to the bridge that goes across the narrow part of the river where the black swans build their nests. Head towards the trees that have those pale pink flowers – not the dark pink ones, though. When you get to the other side of that part of the garden, take the path to the right and follow it until you reach the courtyard – the one that has a row of gardens around the edge where purple flowers are growing. Take the middle path that leads from the courtyard and follow it to the end. That will lead you to the two useful boxes.'

The boy had stood looking at the ground during this rather detailed set of instructions. At each new direction, he nodded his head.

'Got that?' asked Gilliad. The boy nodded again. 'Well,

off you go.'

Latorius shook his head as the boy sped off again.

'What?'

'You know what.'

They sat waiting. Before long, they heard the patter of little sandaled feet on the pavement behind them and a shout of triumph as the boy stumbled upon the two boxes of treasure that had been hiding behind the large trunk of the tree they were sitting under.

'Gave him something to do, didn't it?' said Gilliad, with a wink.

Before they left the children, there was always a story or two, or many, as was usually the case. The children loved stories. Sometimes, Gilliad would tell them stories about the children that he had guarded on the earth. They loved those stories most of all, especially if the story was funny. Sometimes he would make up a story just to entertain and amuse them. Often he would use the children's own names as characters in the story, for he knew all their names. He would pretend it was a coincidence, but it wasn't. He loved to watch their faces if they got a mention. They would sit up straight in surprise.

'That's me!' one would exclaim to all who were listening.

'Really? Are you sure about that?' he would ask, with a twinkle in his eye.

But Gilliad would always take a back seat for the Master Storyteller, for when the Son told a story, Gilliad felt like one of the children, and he would sit at the edge of the crowd – for if the Son was there, the small gathering would be more like a crowd – and he would almost forget where he was, even who he was.

The Son would often visit the children, and He would place them on His knee and tell them of the love of the Father. A large number would gather at His feet and He always had new stories to tell them – parables – stories about things that they understood: the birds, the trees, the animals they cared for. The parables always had messages in them: messages about God's love for them, messages about how they were to live, how they were to treat each other. They would sit quietly listening to the stories, their faces upturned, their eyes fixed on the face of the Son.

When the stories were over, they would lead the Son by the hand. They would show Him the new baby birds, the tiny flower buds that had just begun to burst into bloom, the things they had made. And He would gather a large procession as He walked. They would present Him with tiny gifts – tokens of their love: a small posy of flowers, a colourful drawing of a bird, a garland of interwoven leaves; and He would examine carefully each and every gift, and the giver would feel loved.

And the Son would return to the sanctuary and lay the gifts on the altar – at the feet of their Father – little offerings of thanksgiving, of love.

The Son had not visited the children's paradise for some time now, nor had Gilliad and Latorius seen the Son since they had been on leave, for He had not been present at the banquet, and when they had visited the sanctuary, they had noticed His absence.

Gilliad had not thought about it at the time but, on reflection, he did not remember seeing any of the children's offerings on the altar then either: no tiny posies of flowers, no little bundles of twigs tied up with palm fronds into the shapes of animals and houses.

As they mounted their horses at the gate and strapped on their scabbards, they puzzled over this. Perhaps there was a reason – a logical explanation – Gilliad considered, but, for now, it eluded him.

Chapter Thirteen

It was unusual to be leaving at the same time. Gabriel had summoned Gilliad and Latorius separately to commission them for their next assignments. They were both due to depart shortly and were both to be assigned as guardians. After their briefing, they met in the courtyard near The Great Hall.

'Bethlehem,' they said in unison as soon as they saw each other, and they both laughed. It was not the first time this had happened, nor, they hoped, would it be the last.

The small town of Bethlehem lay just to the south of Jerusalem in an area known for its fertile fields and valleys and was the ancestral home of David, Israel's great king.

Their leave had been much longer than they had expected. Sometimes, the break between assignments was so brief that it seemed like they had barely set foot inside the courtyard when they were being farewelled again.

Once, Gilliad had come across Latorius sitting on one of the stone benches in the courtyard. 'Didn't even know you were here!' he had exclaimed, pleased to see that his friend was on leave at the same time. 'When did you arrive?'

'Just a few moments ago, actually.'

'When are you leaving?'

'In a few moments.'

They were not chosen at random for assignments. Rather, like the guardians in the children's paradise, they were handpicked, the individual character and nature of the angel matched to the person they would be assigned to and the circumstances, and sometimes it just so happened that they were called back to the earth almost immediately. Most of the time, however, they managed to fit in a few training sessions and at least one visit to the children's paradise. And they almost always spent time in the sanctuary.

This time, they had managed to fit in at least a dozen training sessions in the fields as well as several in the space above the heavens. Gilliad's fencing skills had improved, and the last tournament they played, just before their meetings with Gabriel, had seen him declared the winner.

They had played best of three. Latorius had won the first one and Gilliad the second, only by one point, though. They had only intended to play two matches, but Latorius had not wanted to 'leave any unfinished business' – his way of saying that he was sure he would win the next match.

It had been Gilliad's turn to choose the weapon. He chose the heavier sword for the final round. The rules for playing with the heavier sword were slightly different in that you could target anywhere on the body except the head. In the heat of the battle, Latorius had momentarily forgotten this and let his defences down. He had lunged at Gilliad's chest, but Gilliad had managed to deflect the blow by turning swiftly to his side and swinging his sword in an arc pushing Latorius' sword towards the ground, and before Latorius had time to relaunch an attack, Gilliad had landed a sharp jab to his right knee. Point, Gilliad! Match over.

They followed the street from The Great Hall up to the house of the Father.

They left the sanctuary and stood on the steps for a few

moments. It was the final visit before their leave would be over, for Gabriel had informed them that there was a banquet in the making, and once the feasting and the blessings were over, they would depart.

The doors of The Great Hall had not yet opened. They had intended to return to examine the carvings again before they left, at least the ones at the end of the building, and as this seemed like the only opportunity that remained, they made their way along the street towards the building. At least this way they would be close by when the horn sounded, Gilliad thought.

There were a number of others wandering around the building, pausing in front of each door. It was like an outdoor gallery. Works of art; art reflecting life; a shadow of sorts.

As Gilliad and Latorius reached the end of the long building and turned the corner, Latorius ran smack into a marble pedestal on which was balanced a large urn filled with a glossy green-leafed plant. The urn wobbled precariously for a brief moment before toppling over and smashing onto the paving under the column as Latorius jumped back out of the way.

'See, this is why we can't have nice things!' Gilliad had picked that saying up from his last charge, who was always saying this to his brother.

Latorius took a good-natured swipe at his friend, but he ducked in time. He began to pick up the pieces of broken pottery.

'I'll get that,' a voice from behind said.

They hadn't noticed the angel tending to the shrubbery on their right as they came around the end of the building, so intent were they on resuming their examination of the carvings.

Latorius bowed low. 'I would be forever in your debt,' he said. He knew that was not true, however. He just liked to say that. They were always helping each other out, always serving

173

each other.

'Not at all,' replied the gardener. 'You would do the same for me.'

Gallantry, thought Gilliad. That was something that was, generally speaking, missing on earth. People were so self-centred on the whole. And when they did manage to rise above themselves a little, he suspected that it was often just for show.

They wandered along, looking at the doors at the end of the building, stopping at each to examine them closely: carvings of the men of faith – Moses, Joshua, David, and many others – men chosen by God – part of His great plan for the salvation of mankind.

On one of the doors there was a carving of The Ten Commandments and Gilliad read these aloud. These had been written on tablets of stone by the Lord's own finger and given to Moses and the Israelites. And there were many other laws, too.

'The people would have kept out of a lot of unnecessary trouble if they had only kept these laws,' Gilliad observed.

'Easier said than done,' said Latorius. 'They are sinners by nature, remember.'

That they are, thought Gilliad, nodding in agreement. That they are.

The people continually failed at keeping the Law. In fact, none of them managed to keep the whole Law. But the Law served a purpose, for the knowledge of sin caused the people to feel guilt in their hearts. The people did not like this feeling of guilt – this feeling of an unclean heart – and the unwelcome feeling of guilt caused the people to feel the need to confess their sins and to seek forgiveness.

The law of sin and death required that sin be paid for by death. Under the Law, the people were required to sacrifice an animal as payment for their sins. The people would come to the tabernacle bearing an offering – an animal for sacrifice –

usually a lamb or a goat without defect or blemish. The priest would then present the offering on behalf of the people and the guilt of the person would be symbolically transferred by the laying of the priest's hands on the animal and the penalty of God's wrath for sin – death – the shedding of blood – was transferred to the animal. The people's sins were then covered, the Lord would forgive their sins, and their hearts would be cleansed from unrighteousness.

But it was not the sacrifice that cleansed the hearts of the people. The sacrifice needed to be accompanied by repentance and faith, and then God would forgive the people their sins. The sacrifices were only effective if offered in faith: faith that God would forgive their sins; faith in the mercy of God and in the coming Messiah who would put an end to these sacrifices.

And because the people had faith in God for the forgiveness of sins, He gave them His righteousness. It was an exchange, for the people had no righteousness of their own.

It was an unfair exchange, Gilliad had often thought: an exchange of something bad for something good; the exchange of the guilt and the unrighteousness of the sinner for the righteousness of God.

But God also required something of the people. Just as sacrifice was not a substitute for repentance and faith, neither was it a substitute for obedience. Above sacrifice and burnt offerings, the Lord required love and the knowledge of Him. Obedience was a demonstration of the people's faith in God and of their love for God, and at this the people often fell short.

The land of Canaan, which God had given the Israelites, was already occupied by other nations when the people crossed into it, led by Joshua – wicked nations who worshipped idols and even sacrificed their own children. With the help of the Lord and more than a little help from the angels, thought Gilliad, as he recalled the battle scenes that were depicted on the door, these nations were driven out.

As the Israelites battled the people who occupied the land of Canaan, a spiritual war was also waged, for Canaan was a major demonic stronghold. Under the archangel Michael, who was the protector of the chosen people, all leagues who were not currently on assignment were called to rally to keep the enemy at bay.

One of the first fortified cities of Canaan to be toppled was Jericho, and on the way to Jericho, the Lord allowed Joshua to see the commander of the army of the Lord, so that he would know that the people were not fighting the battle in their own strength.

There had been a number of other times when the angels were allowed to be seen. Once, when the Israelites were facing the enemy, the eyes of a servant of the prophet Elisha were opened, and he was able to see that the mountains around God's people were filled with horses and chariots of fire, for there was a mighty heavenly army on their side. The heavenly army fought side by side with the people, and victory was theirs. The people were not alone.

They moved on to the door depicting the reign of King David. The people enjoyed peace for a time under David's reign and also under the reign of his son, Solomon. David had made Jerusalem the nation's capital, and under Solomon, the nation prospered and became powerful.

Solomon extended the city and built a temple in which the people could worship God. He engaged in extensive foreign trade and the nation was well regarded amongst its neighbours. But the people were oppressed with forced labour and heavily taxed. After Solomon's death, they appealed to the new king, Rehoboam, the son of Solomon, to lighten their burdens, but he refused.

The ten northern tribes rebelled and set themselves up as a separate kingdom, which was called Israel. They had their own king and their own capital at Shechem. David's successors continued to rule the two tribes of the southern kingdom, known as Judah, from Jerusalem. But the division weakened the two kingdoms and they became more vulnerable to invasions and attacks by other powerful nations.

Throughout the years, the people were often unfaithful to the Lord, at times even taking on the idolatrous practices of the nations around them. But God continued to show His love for them, sending many prophets to warn the people to turn from their sins. The people did not always heed these warnings, and often they paid the price for disobedience, sometimes by bringing disasters upon themselves and upon the land – plagues and droughts. But despite the influence of false religions, invasion by other nations, exile in foreign countries, and worldly influences, there had always been a remnant that remained faithful to God; to His Word.

God had given the people His written Word. The Scriptures were the people's history – their story. The Scriptures told the people of the Creation and of God's love for them. Through the prophets, God had told the people of the coming of the Messiah and the words of these prophecies were written in the Holy Scriptures to be preserved and passed down through the generations – words of hope.

According to the ancient prophecy in the Garden of Eden, the Messiah would be born of the Seed of the woman only. The prophets said that He would be born in Bethlehem, the city of King David, and would be from the royal line of David, descended from the line of Judah.

The Messiah would be ruler in Israel – a king – a redeemer who would set the people free, and he would come to those who repent of their sins. He would bring salvation, healing, and freedom, and he would wipe out the covenant of death.

Although there had been those who, at various times, thought the Messiah had come, even those who thought they were the Messiah, the people were still waiting. The prophecies were specific, and many scholars over the years had studied these, trying to determine when the Messiah would come.

And the people had looked for this king. And they kept looking. And every generation waited in hope.

But one thing Gilliad knew with certainty was that the enemy did not understand the prophecies for, time and again, Satan had tried to prevent the words of the prophets from being fulfilled.

Time and again, he had failed.

He would always fail, Gilliad thought, for God keeps His promises, and His promise was to send the Messiah.

Chapter Fourteen

The courtyard was full. The steps of the sanctuary from which they had just descended were crowded. It seemed as if the whole complement of those who were on leave had assembled to see them off.

The feast had ended with some hearty singing and even a little impromptu dancing by those less inclined to decorum, including Latorius. The feasts were always punctuated by spontaneous performances, mostly by the poets among them who would suddenly leap up onto their chairs and spout something deep and meaningful before resuming their places and carrying on with their meal.

Sometimes, the floor would be taken by those with a leaning towards comedy, and the hall would burst into peals of laughter. Occasionally, a scholarly angel, although more usually an archangel, would rise ceremoniously from his seat and offer a riddle. Everyone would sit for a while in silence, trying to fathom the answer, trying to be the first to break the code or solve the puzzle, and the scholar would watch the faces of those around him. It was usually the same ones each time who came up with the answers.

This time, Gilliad had actually thought he knew the answer to one of the riddles offered. He had thought for a few moments, weighing up possibilities, and then, when he was feeling confident with the answer he had decided on, he pushed his chair out from the table to stand up. But he was stuck fast, for someone had tied his sash to the leg of the chair. He bent down and started to struggle with the knot, but he was all thumbs, and before he had managed to remedy the situation, the answer had been given by another. Point Latorius! Payback, no doubt, for Gilliad switching sauces on him moments earlier, which was payback for Latorius hiding a small child in the supposedly empty useful box that Gilliad bent down to pick up when they were leaving the children's paradise, initially causing Gilliad to wonder if, somehow, he had lost a little of his strength and, moments later, startling him and causing him to almost drop the box, child and all.

No matter, he thought, with some measure of relief. His answer was a long way off the mark.

Occasionally, it happened that no one knew the answer. Sometimes the banquet would draw to a close and Gilliad would be left in suspense. The riddle would then play on his mind. These unanswered riddles, though, gave him something to think about during the quiet moments – the long nights when he was on assignment.

He had been on assignment in Bethlehem before, several times in fact, and he had seen many changes in the religious, cultural, and political climate over the centuries in Palestine, as the land of Canaan was now called.

Kings and empires had come and gone since the reign of Saul, David, and Solomon, and the two kingdoms – Israel and Judah – had remained divided.

The Assyrians had held domination over that part of the world for some seven hundred years. The Assyrian army had been ruthless. They burnt cities, even children, impaled victims on stakes, beheaded others, and chopped hands off others, having little regard for human life, and their conquest of surrounding territories had been relentless.

The Assyrian king had defeated the northern kingdom of Israel after a lengthy siege, carrying away thousands of Israelites and settling them in other parts of the Assyrian Empire, bringing to an end the northern kingdom. Most of these captives had never returned and they had been replaced with strangers from far away.

The Assyrian army had later overrun Judah, besieging and conquering numerous towns and capturing many thousands of Jews. The Assyrians had planned an attack on Jerusalem, but God had intervened on behalf of His chosen people and the angel of the Lord had struck down one hundred and eighty-five thousand Assyrian soldiers. The king of Assyria was forced to retreat.

Finally, the Babylonians took the Assyrian city of Nineveh, and Babylonian independence was won from Assyria replacing it as the new world power. The Babylonians overpowered the kingdom of Judah, destroying Jerusalem. They burnt down the magnificent temple built by King Solomon, seizing anything of value that they could carry away, and they forced the people into captivity in Babylon leaving only the poorest farm workers.

During the southern tribes' seventy-year captivity, the Persians conquered Babylon and the Babylonians passed from the scene as a world power. The Persian kings extended their borders even further than previous empires and divided the empire into provinces, each with its own ruler. The new empire created great wealth and many craftsmen were brought from every part of the empire to decorate the new palaces and other buildings.

The Persian king, Cyrus, allowed his subject people to retain their religion and culture and he issued a decree to restore the Jews to their homeland. Small numbers of the people returned to Jerusalem – a remnant. Under the Persian Empire, the restoration of Jerusalem was commenced and the rebuilding of the Jewish temple was decreed.

During Persian rule, the Greeks had struggled for

supremacy. Eventually, Alexander the Great swept across countries conquering all in his path, including Palestine, and the rule of the Persians, which had lasted some two hundred years, was taken over by the conquering and powerful Greek Empire.

The Greeks were a proud people with a great love of freedom and they thought of themselves as different from other races – more cultured, more intelligent, more enlightened, and Alexander set about spreading Greek civilisation throughout the entire area and making Greek the dominant language. They built many cities throughout the empire and large numbers of Greeks moved out of the overpopulated and unsustaining country of Greece. They began to populate the other countries that had been taken over by the empire, including the tiny land of Palestine.

The Romans, whose power had increased, finally ended Greek rule. The whole Mediterranean area, including the part of Palestine to the north, which was now called Galilee, as well as Samaria and Judea, as the southern parts of the Promised Land were now known, now came under Roman authority.

After many years of war, the Roman emperor, Augustus, had united the whole of the Mediterranean world under one somewhat peaceful government.

By the time Gilliad and Latorius had returned to heaven from their last assignments, the Romans had been in power for some sixty years. Like the Grecian Empire, Roman rule had brought law, order, and stability, but the Romans maintained the peace by garrisons of soldiers and the people were heavily taxed.

The Romans had retained the Greek language, and the arts, music, literature, and architecture had continued to flourish. But along with the decadence, prosperity, and progress had come moral degeneration. The people were self-centred, self-indulgent, and greedy, thinking only of themselves: of their happiness, their wealth, their importance.

The land of the chosen people, from which Gilliad and Latorius had recently returned, was now awash with a conglomeration of religions and beliefs; remnants of pagan beliefs from the ancient cultures into which the chosen people had been assimilated during their periods of exile, as well as beliefs that had been brought in by those who had replaced them.

There remained within Palestine both Assyrian and Babylonian beliefs and these pagan practices intertwined with the more recent influx of Greek and Roman gods.

Many people had turned to astrology and magic, believing that the planets and stars governed the lives and the fate of humans. Still others turned to the new religions that had come from the people of the east. Many of these new religions appealed to the people, for they promised a personal salvation to the worshipper; some promising to save them from evil, trouble or danger; some promising success in life in return for the devotion of the worshipper.

Some of these new religions even promised to save the worshipper from death, and this appealed to the hearts of many, for to be free from the fear of death, their greatest enemy, was their deepest desire. But it was an empty promise, for no one had returned from the gates of death, and their fear remained.

Others turned from religion to philosophy to try and fill the emptiness in their hearts, to dispel the confusion in their minds, and their desire became simply to live in harmony with reason and to live a quiet life without fear, but deep in their hearts, the fear of death remained.

Many people simply dabbled in whatever they thought might bring them good luck, peace, good health and wealth in this life, and immortality in the next. But the religion of the Greeks and Romans and the other false religions that abounded in the land of Palestine did not offer the people answers to the problems of good and evil and the questions of life and death. These false gods – these demons masquerading as gods – could not save them from the curse of death; neither could the stars or the oracles; neither could their philosophers. The people were confused. Many were searching for the truth; many of the people were in despair.

Whilst there was still a remnant of the chosen people who had remained faithful to the one true God, even they were often in opposition to each other. Under both Greek and Roman rule, the Sanhedrin – the Jewish court that was ruled by a Jewish high priest and his council – had been allowed a measure of self-rule as long as they paid taxes and abided by the Roman general's rules. However, disputes often broke out between the members: the Pharisees or scribes, some of whom were also priests, and the Sadducees, who were chief priests and elders.

The Pharisees, whilst being committed to keeping the Law, had made the traditions surrounding the Law almost as important as the Law itself, and whilst they observed the Law carefully, their hearts were often far from God and their motives wrong, for they desired human praise and trusted in their own righteousness. They looked down on such 'sinners' as tax collectors and prostitutes, as well as those who, in their eyes, did not keep God's Law, failing to see that in God's eyes they themselves were sinners too.

The Sadducees, on the other hand, insisted that only the Law of Moses was binding, but many of the Sadducees had become corrupt and the people had begun to lose respect for their teachings.

Unlike the Pharisees, the Sadducees did not believe in life after death, or in angels or spirits, and Latorius, at the risk of receiving 'the eyebrow' from Arkellus, would often make it his business to go right up to the face of a Sadducee and say: 'I don't believe in Sadducees', just because he could.

Gilliad, whilst amused by this, tended to show greater restraint; although, once in a while, he had thought about suddenly materialising right in front of them; perhaps sitting himself down in the midst of one of their heated debates and then suddenly appearing. That would be satisfying, he thought. But … rules are rules.

And it was to this climate of political rule, this religious conglomeration, this cultural melting pot: a mix of Greeks, Romans, and Jews, as well as a myriad of other nationalities, that Gilliad and Latorius were about to return.

Bethlehem was normally a busy bustling town, but it would be even busier than usual on their return, with noisy jostling people from many different nationalities, many different religions and languages, all looking for places to stay, for during their time of leave, the Roman emperor, Caesar Augustus, had issued a decree that all persons within the bounds of the Roman Empire, including those in the town of Bethlehem in the province of Judea in Palestine, must register in their home towns for a census.

Gilliad and Latorius stood near the massive iridescent pearly gate through which they were to descend. The archangel Gabriel had, moments before, descended the sanctuary steps, and as the crowds of well-wishers had parted, had made his way towards them, causing a gradual hush to descend over the crowd of heavenly hosts.

It was unusual to be seen off by Gabriel, and they bowed their heads to acknowledge the great honour that he was bestowing upon them by his presence.

He stood in front of them for a long moment before he began his blessing, and looked from one to the other and nodded. Yes, he thought, well chosen.

'Gilliad, gentle protector and faithful servant, and Latorius, loyal and trustworthy,' he began. He placed his hands on each of their heads, and unfortunately for Gilliad, who badly needed to make one last point, knocked off the small flower that he had, with impressive stealth, managed to insert into the wiry curls on the back of Latorius' mess of hair while they were waiting on the bench.

He watched it flutter to the ground. No matter.

'It is the Father's request,' Gabriel continued, 'that I confer upon you His blessing as you leave to embark upon your next mission. You have proven that your sole purpose is to do the will of the Father. You have demonstrated discernment between right and wrong, and in all things and at all times shown wisdom, always doing what is right in the eyes of the Lord. For this reason, the Father has chosen you for this mission. May His Holy Spirit guide you and keep you within His will, and may you bring glory to His name as you go forth into the world below.'

They took one last glance at their heavenly home, at their family who had come to see them off, and stepped out of the light and into the darkness below, first Latorius, then Gilliad, after looking behind briefly to check the back of his robe. No ... no reed this time!

The echoes of angelic singing quickly dissipated as they descended rapidly through the vastness of space past constellations and planets as they hurtled towards the earth before breaking through the light blanket of cloud above the gently flickering pinpricks of light that glowed in the stillness of the night over the sleepy little town of Bethlehem.

Part Four

Chapter Fifteen

They touched down in an open field on the outskirts of the town of Bethlehem; Gilliad with his usual controlled style of landing, Latorius exercising his trademark crash-land, forward roll, re-balance, both feet splayed at an odd angle style of landing.

Whatever makes you happy, thought Gilliad, shaking his head.

They made their way towards the lights of the town along a narrow path which meandered its way between long grass. The path had been trodden into a hard, almost rock-like, surface over the centuries. The land around was fertile and ideal for grazing, and the path served as a thoroughfare for shepherds and their flocks.

There were sheep everywhere in Palestine. In fact, on almost every available green hill and valley one could find a shepherd tending his flock. Most of the flocks were owned and tended to by several members of the one family, each shepherd taking his watch, protecting the sheep from marauding wild animals. Occasionally, though, there would be two or three shepherds tending to a larger flock, and it was common to see a father and his young sons camped out for the night beside the flock, the young apprentices learning the language of the sheep; learning how to build the flock's trust in them; learning how to keep them safe.

There were many dangers in the hills: wolves, lions, bears, and snakes, and sheep were easily frightened. The shepherd had to constantly be on guard and he had to learn the art of sleeping lightly. 'Sleep with one eye open,' the fathers would advise their young sons.

Shepherding was usually passed down from father to son and the flock was part of the son's inheritance. A good steward of the flock would build up the numbers of sheep over his lifetime so that he would have a sizable flock to split between his sons, at least the ones who were interested in continuing the tradition.

Keeping sheep, while not the most profitable occupation, usually brought in sufficient income to keep the family comfortable. The ewes were milked once a day and the milk was sold at the markets. Mutton was eaten regularly by most families as it was readily available and affordable to most. Sometimes, the women would barter at the markets, swapping the milk or mutton for household items that they needed: oil for lamps, wheat, honey, or salt. Often, there were days when they would go to the markets with their wares and no money would change hands, but they would come home laden with all kinds of goods. Sometimes, they would have bargained for a service; perhaps even help with shearing.

The sheep were herded into an enclosure and shorn once a year. This was in the spring when their coats had grown thick and they were starting to feel the heat of the midday sun. Shearing time was quite an occasion amongst the shepherds. Throughout the year, they mostly led a solitary life, the sheep being their only company for much of the time. Although they could usually see other shepherds on the hills, unless they happened to pass them as they herded their flock from one area to the next, their contact was often little more than a wave.

At shearing time, however, a large enclosure would be

set up close to the outskirts of town and several families would bring their flocks to be shorn. Often they would employ men and boys from the town, and at the end of each day of shearing, the women in the family would prepare a large feast and the shearers and their families would sit around a crackling fire and eat and sing and tell stories. The children would run around until they were exhausted, and then they would flop down on the grass and watch the stars until they were no longer able to keep their eyes open, and gradually the camp would grow quiet.

The nights would always seem short at shearing time, partly because the sun was beginning to set later and rise earlier, but mostly because the shepherds and their families had looked forward to this event all year and it was over too soon. When the first rays of the sun began to shine on the sleepy little camp, the whole process would start all over again.

There were jobs for everyone: food to prepare, bedding to roll up, and, most importantly, sheep to be shorn.

During the busy shearing time in the spring, the wool from the sheep was sold at the markets cleaned and carded ready for spinning and weaving, or straight off the sheep's back, saving the seller time and the purchaser money. At other times during the year, the wool was made into garments by the wives, daughters, and sisters of the shepherds. They would make warm hats that came right down over the ears and had flaps that extended down the back of the neck. These were very popular at the markets for they were perfect for the shepherds to wear out in the fields at night when the bitterly cold wind blew from the west over the Mediterranean Sea and made its way across the coastal plains and up into the hills or whipped mercilessly through the valleys where the sheep grazed.

The women also made undergarments of very finely spun wool, and the mothers of the young boys who went out with their fathers to tend the flocks would always insist that they wore these somewhat scratchy and uncomfortable items of clothing under their linen tunics. 'Always dress from the

191

inside out, son,' the mothers would say. 'There is no point in wearing only a warm outer garment if the wind is whipping up a storm under your tunic!' And the boys would roll their eyes when their mothers' backs were turned. But when they were out on the fields on a cold winter's night, they would be grateful they had followed their advice.

Along the path a little way, Gilliad and Latorius came across a small group of shepherds. They were standing close to a fire in the centre of a clearing, their sheep huddled under a copse of trees nearby. The sheep were quiet, content after a day of grazing.

The two angels took their places around the fire with the men. They liked to listen in to conversations. It provided a never-ending source of entertainment. The shepherds, of course, remained oblivious to the intrusion. Gilliad was not so sure about the sheep, however, as a number of them had begun shuffling about and quietly bleating.

'Hush, hush,' the older boy called, wandering over to the flock. They soon quietened again, and he returned to his father and brother who were deep in conversation with two slightly weather-beaten shepherds who had camped in the same area for the night.

The younger boy, Gilliad noticed, had begun staring in his direction. Gilliad looked at Latorius.

'What?'

Latorius just grinned.

Gilliad knew what that meant. Point Latorius.

He had checked the back of his tunic already. He ran his hands quickly through his hair. He watched the boy's face as his eyes followed the feather that fluttered to the ground.

The boy walked around to the other side of the fire to investigate and bent down to retrieve the feather.

'What are you doing lad?' asked the father.

'This fell from the sky ...' began the boy.

'It's a feather. Feathers usually fall from the sky.'

The boy tucked it in the pocket of his tunic.

Latorius added a mark to his invisible tally.

'Again, won on a technicality,' said Gilliad.

'A win by any other name is still a win,' Latorius retorted.

There were a number of other small fires visible on the hills around them. The wind had dropped and the smoke from the fires rose in hazy columns high into the still night air. The light cloud cover had lifted now and the stars shone brightly in the black sky.

There was a new star in the heavens, or at least that is what the older shepherds thought. They had been staring up into the sky most nights since they were boys and neither of them remembered seeing this star before. It was almost directly overhead and much brighter than all the rest.

It intrigued the younger boy, and he stood with his head back and mouth open for a long time, just staring into the sky.

'You'll catch a fly if you're not careful.'

His father placed one hand on the top of the boy's head and the other under his chin and the boy's teeth snapped together. He sat himself on the ground near the sheep and brushed away several sticks and stones before lying on his back. He didn't know much about stars, but the new star fascinated him, and he listened as his father and the older shepherds debated what this meant.

'I have seen stars shooting across the sky before, but have never seen a new star appear,' said one.

'Perhaps it is a star that had been there all the time and we did not notice,' said the other.

'I don't think so.'

'Could it be a star that was there all along but has become brighter for some reason?'

The other shepherd stood for some time stroking his long white beard, contemplating this possibility. 'I don't know,' he said, eventually. 'I have not known of this happening before and I have been staring at the night sky since before you were crawling.'

The other shepherd snorted at this. They were brothers, advanced in their years but, nevertheless, only a year apart. Both were prone to exaggeration.

The father of the boys had been listening to the exchange between the brothers and had not thought it wise to offer his opinion. He respected the older shepherds for their wisdom and experience. But while they had been debating the possibilities of whether this was a new star or an old star that, for some reason, had decided to shine more brightly than all the rest, he had been trying to recall a conversation that he had overheard whilst in the synagogue some years ago.

He had brought his family in to worship one Sabbath, as was his usual habit. On the way out, he had overheard two scribes debating a passage of the Holy Scriptures that spoke of a star that would appear in the sky. It was part of an oracle, if he remembered rightly.

'I have heard,' began the father, 'that there will be a star that will come out of Jacob. Perhaps this could be it.'

The two older men looked at the younger man with interest. He knew that they were expecting him to say more but, in truth, that was all he knew. He was amazed that he had even remembered that much, but it was something that had stuck in his mind. His wife was always reminding him of how little seemed to stick. 'Have you paid the men for helping with the shearing yet? Have you remembered to buy new baskets for the wool to be taken to the markets in? Have you remembered where you put the money that you made from the sale of the mutton? Have you ... have you ...' It wasn't his fault that he forgot things all the time. He had a lot on his mind after all. All she had to do was run the household. How hard could that be?

The older men were waiting expectantly for him to

continue.

'I really don't know any more than that. It was just something I heard the scribes at the synagogue talking about.'

'Perhaps it is a sign of something,' the older one offered. 'The Creator puts signs in the heavens, does he not?'

'Indeed He does. Perhaps that is what it is then.'

They unrolled their bedding around the campfire. They would take it in turns to keep watch over the sheep. It was unusual to have help with the night watch but it would be nice to at least be able to sleep soundly for part of the night without having to be on constant alert. As there were two fairly large flocks between them to watch over, at least two of them would have to stay awake.

The father walked over to where the younger boy had lain down. It had been a busy day and, not surprisingly, he did not stir. He wandered back to where the others were arranging their mats.

'We'll take the second watch,' he said, pointing his thumb in the direction of his sleeping son. The old shepherds nodded.

The father and the older son lay down on their bed rolls. The boy stared up at the sky for a few moments, then, like his brother, his eyelids grew heavy and he drifted off into a peaceful sleep.

The father lay awake. The bedding was thin and he could feel lumps from several stubborn clumps of grass. He had tried to pull them out, but they had been stuck fast in the hard ground. It was all right for these young ones, he thought, they could sleep through anything. He remembered a time not long ago, or so it seemed, when he would not even bother half the time to unroll his mat. But he was not as young as he used to be and his joints often ached, especially in the early hours of the morning. Sometimes, he felt he could do with several rolls of bedding. Occasionally, if his sons did not bother to use theirs, he would sleep on a double or triple mat.

The more comfortable he was, however, the harder it was to begin his watch.

The older shepherds sat quietly beside the fire warming their hands. Even though the days were still warm, a chill had crept into the air with the arrival of dusk.

Gilliad and Latorius left the shepherds and continued on their way. They too were aware of the prophecy of the star, for it was written in one of the large volumes that graced the shelves in the common room.

'My guess would be that it is a new star,' Latorius said, as they followed the pathway in and out between low bushes.

'But,' said Gilliad, 'when the Creator had finished creating, He really had finished.'

'Good point.'

'Perhaps then, as the old man said, it is a star that had been there all along but, for some reason, is now shining brighter than before.'

They neared the outskirts of the town. It was still fairly early in the evening and from most of the houses there were lights glowing through open windows or filtering through shutters.

The poorer people, who lived on the outskirts of the town in tiny houses that often consisted only of a couple of rooms, left lighting their lamps until the last possible moment in order to economise on oil. It was not unusual to see them through windows or out in their tiny yards attending to their chores in almost total darkness, peering closely at whatever it was they were doing, feeling their way along the sides of houses, setting tables for the evening meal almost by touch alone. When they finally did light a lamp, there was only one lit for the entire family, and it was not left burning for longer than was necessary.

'Early to bed tonight,' the mothers would say. And the children would protest and complain loudly. Their heads would barely have touched their bedding when the lamp would be blown out and all would be in darkness. But they knew they had to ration the oil or there would be nights when they would be in bed even earlier.

As they moved towards the centre of town, the houses were slightly larger, the occupants a little wealthier, and the lights would go on earlier and burn brighter and longer. Some houses boasted a lamp in every room and, as they passed, they could hear the sounds of mothers clearing up from the evening meal, fathers telling stories to the children of their days out in the fields, in the blacksmith shops, or out fishing in the tiny river that ran close to Bethlehem and emptied into the Dead Sea. And they could hear children singing and babies crying, refusing to settle for the night.

The smells of evening meals drifted out through the windows and Gilliad, who considered that his nose had, by now, perfected the ability to distinguish between various aromas, especially if those aromas pertained to food, gave a running commentary as they passed each house.

They passed through streets where everyone seemed to be cooking with the same spices. New settlers in Palestine tended to congregate with their own. This often meant that everyone in a particular area ate from a distinct cuisine – a diet made up of the foods that they were most familiar with, using traditional recipes and cooking styles that they had brought with them.

'Garlic … lots of garlic with a touch of onion. Something pungent … let me think … ah, yes: lemon with a hint of horseradish. Not sure if that's a good combination! Ah, now I know that smell!' A sweet smell of honey drifted out from one of the windows where a young woman was stirring a large pot from which steam was gently rising. 'Someone's having a treat tonight!' They continued on down the street. 'Meat … let me think … fowl, no wait … lamb, definitely lamb. With rosemary,' he added.

He prided himself on being specific. He was rarely wrong. He had once wrapped his sash around his eyes when they were in The Great Hall at one of the banquets, and he had asked Latorius to present him with as many different fruits, herbs, spices, nuts, and vegetables as he could. He rarely had to try something more than once. One mouthful and he could pick what it was.

The others at the table had joined in. And he never missed a beat. No sooner was the food in his mouth and he could name it. He was so quick that the other angels had begun to chorus 'don't talk with your mouth full!' each time he answered. He then had to try to refrain from saying the answer until he had swallowed. That was hard.

After a while, they had decided that it was not a challenge for him to name single foods, so they started offering him foods that had been prepared with a number of ingredients. Still that did not stump him, and eventually they had conceded defeat. He was applauded loudly at the end but, being the humble angel that he was, he had simply nodded at his audience and said, 'I guess we are all gifted in different ways.' He was not sure of the exact purpose of that particular gift. Perhaps it would be revealed to him in time.

They saw a woman standing under the overhang of roof at the back of her house. The fence was high but they could easily see over it, and they stood for a while watching her as she ran a knife along the side of a huge fish and began methodically removing its insides.

'Large family,' commented Gilliad. He could hear several children squabbling inside the house. 'Not surprised she is outside!'

The smell that drifted through the window of the next house they passed emitted a strong odour of which hints of it had met them several houses back.

'Kidneys,' Latorius offered. 'Even I can pick that one!' He wrinkled his nose. 'Why on earth would anyone want to eat kidneys? Do they even realise what the kidney has been up to before they eat it?'

Gilliad laughed. 'It's probably the cleanest organ in the sheep.'

'Even so ...'

The centre of the town was busy. There were people milling around looking for places to stay – couples, families with children, others on their own – all looking for a bed for the night. Those who had arrived several days ago had had their choice of inns, and those who had not had the forethought to arrive early for the census were the ones with the slight look of anxiety on their faces, for there was precious little available, not even on the outskirts of town or in some of the less desirable inns.

They could see innkeepers beginning to turn their signs around and tired parents with overexcited children clinging to their legs were beginning to despair.

The markets had stayed open into the evening, vendors taking advantage of the influx of visitors to the town, and some of the families had resigned themselves to waiting out the night in the market square, just grateful for a bite to eat and a doorstep on which to arrange their mats. Some of the children had already fallen asleep, propped up against walls and doorways next to their parents, exhausted from the long dusty journey.

'We must have been given a child to guard in the same area,' observed Gilliad, as they continued to head in the same direction.

That was not altogether unusual. In fact, it had happened several times. That was nice, Gilliad thought. He liked to think that Latorius was somewhere nearby. They liked each other's company and, although it was not the same as when their leave happened to coincide, there would still be the chance, however slight, that they might run into each other.

'I'm only following the coordinates Gabriel gave me. They must be very similar to yours,' said Latorius.

'Indeed they must,' agreed Gilliad.

199

J R Thomas

They were almost at the end of their journey. They turned down a small alleyway, paved in uneven cobblestone. It was narrow and dark, lit only by the scattered shards of light from the cracks of some of the shuttered windows. Ahead of them was an old grey donkey led by a young man. Its hooves clopped loudly on the cobblestones, and the echoes bounced off the stone walls of the inns on either side.

There was a small figure sitting on the back of the plodding donkey, wrapped tightly in a thin woollen blanket to keep out the cold. A women, thought Gilliad.

As the young man approached a door which was set back in the wall, a short rotund man wearing a dirty striped apron and carrying what looked like a stick, stepped out onto the front step. He reached up with the stick and removed the sign that hung sideways from a small black iron frame, replacing it with another.

The young man's shoulders drooped. He hailed the man as he turned to step back into the inn, and Gilliad listened as he pleaded with the innkeeper to let them stay for the night. They had travelled for days to get to Bethlehem and they were desperate.

'Everyone's desperate,' Gilliad heard the innkeeper say.

He watched as the woman got slowly down from the donkey and tried to stand up straight. She put her shoulders back and let out a cry.

The innkeeper looked her up and down. 'Oh,' he said, stroking his long beard.

There were a few muffled exchanges, but eventually the innkeeper gestured to the young man to continue on around the corner.

The man led the donkey, holding the hand of the woman, who was now moaning softly. The innkeeper went back inside and bolted the door, and Gilliad and Latorius continued walking down the alleyway.

'Poor things,' said Gilliad.

They stopped at the closed door.

'Well, I think this is where I will have to leave you, my friend,' said Gilliad.

Latorius had opened his mouth to say the same thing. 'But this is where I am supposed to begin my assignment.'

They both looked at each other. Gabriel never made a mistake. If this was where he had told them both to go, then this was where they were both supposed to be.

They passed through the door.

The inn, as the innkeeper had told the young couple, was certainly full.

They passed a large table laden with food. Gilliad had never seen so many people standing or sitting around one table. There were children everywhere, and they nodded to the other guardians as they passed. There were arms and legs everywhere, people reaching over other people for food, parents yelling at children or trying to find little ones who had escaped their watchful, or not so watchful, eyes.

The innkeeper's wife's face was red and sweat trickled down the sides. She had never had to cater for this many guests before. But, she tried to remind herself, it was all money, and they definitely needed money. Although, right at that moment, she wondered if it was really worth it, for she felt like her head was about to burst, it ached so, not to mention her legs.

They continued through to the back door of the inn. There was a strong smell of hay and manure coming from across the small yard, and they could hear the sound of a cow and at least one or two sheep. The donkey that they had seen earlier was now standing with its head buried in a large tub of loose hay.

Good, thought Gilliad, at least the young couple seem to have found a place for the night, although he had not noticed them inside the inn. Perhaps the innkeeper had given them a small room somewhere away from the rabble then. Just as well, he thought. He had noticed, as the woman had rounded the corner of the building, that she was heavy with child. Not a good time to be travelling. But everyone had to register. No exceptions, they had been told.

Perhaps one of them would be assigned to the newborn child of this woman, Gilliad thought, but they had both been given coordinates that were beyond the inn, so they continued walking through the yard, past the donkey.

Latorius blew into the donkey's ear as they passed it and gave it a quick pat on the rump. The donkey didn't flinch. Sometimes, animals were enabled to see, hear, or feel the angels, but more often than not, they weren't. Everything had a purpose and, much to Latorius' disappointment, but not to his surprise, there was absolutely no purpose in startling the donkey. Entertainment was not considered a purpose. More's the pity, he thought.

On the other side of the yard there was a stable. Like the yard, it was small; built to accommodate only a few animals. Many of the inns in Bethlehem had such stables out the back. The fowls provided eggs for the table and one cow or a couple of sheep provided sufficient milk for an average number of guests, as well as the family of the innkeeper.

They passed through a slatted wooden gate which hung precariously from its hinges. The entire stable, in fact, had seen better days and was in need of a coat of paint and some major repairs. The animals, while probably warmer in the stable than out in the yard, would certainly not be snug in here on a cold winter's night, thought Gilliad, for the gaps between the boards and where the walls met the dirt floor were large enough to let in drafts.

They could hear the sounds of the animals shuffling around in the cramped stalls as they passed.

'Perhaps we are to be guardians of animals this time!' said Latorius.

Gilliad snorted – a sound, to Latorius' amusement, not

unlike those the animals were making – and he rolled his eyes. They had never been given the wrong coordinates. Wherever they were headed, it was in the right direction.

They passed a cow that had settled down onto the straw that lined her small enclosure. At least, Gilliad assumed the cow was lying on straw, but there was so little space left around her that it was difficult to tell. She lay with her legs folded under her, contentedly chewing her cud.

Opposite the cow was a stall of roughly the same size. In this stall there were two sheep jostling for space, bumping up against the sides of the stall and bleating at each other in annoyance. They could hear clucking noises coming from what appeared to be the main open area of the stable and they could hear the voice of a man: a man talking in quiet soothing tones. And as they rounded the corner, they saw the young woman, and her time had come.

Chapter Sixteen

The young woman was half lying, half sitting on the woollen blanket she had been wrapped in for their long journey. The man had managed to push as much loose straw as he could find into a pile, but even so, it did little to cushion the hard ground. The woman had settled herself down on the straw as soon as they had been shown into the stable and there she had stayed.

They had travelled from the town of Nazareth, in Galilee, to Bethlehem, the man's home town. He was a descendant of the house of David, as was the woman, who was pledged in marriage to him.

'Twins,' announced Gilliad.

'I don't think so,' said Latorius. 'She hardly looks big enough for one baby, let alone two.'

'Then why would we both be here?'

'You have a point.' He still did not see how it could possibly be two, but there was no point in debating something they would soon know anyway.

They sat down in the corner on a large bale of hay which was tied tightly with twine. It would be a while, according to Latorius.

'I still think you are wrong,' he said. He rather fancied himself an expert in the field of childbirth. He had attended numerous births; they both had. Every time they were sent on guardian assignment for a child, they would be commissioned before the child was born; often hours before, for sometimes the birth was long and drawn out.

Latorius had taken to coaching the woman through the whole process. She couldn't hear him, of course, but that didn't stop him. Besides, he rather thought he knew more than the Hebrew midwives.

Gilliad had seen him in action once. That time, they actually had both been assigned to twins. There were two midwives in attendance – competent, experienced women with more than a few deliveries between them. They were the midwives who, if anything was difficult, or if anything was likely to go wrong, the mothers could do no better than to have these women by their sides.

But, of course, Latorius knew better.

Gilliad had leant up against a wall or sat on the floor for the duration of the birth, knowing that there was no point in doing much else. They were not to interfere anyway.

Latorius, on the other hand, had acted like he was the third midwife, darting back and forth, yelling out orders, calling out: 'Push, push! Don't push! Push now!' and all manner of instructions. Of course, no one took any notice of someone they could neither see nor hear.

In the end, the babies were born strong and healthy, and Latorius had straightened up, stretched his arms, and breathed a great sigh of relief as the midwives held them upside down and the babies had proceeded to let the whole neighbourhood know of their arrival.

He had walked over to Gilliad and shaken his hand.

'We have two boys,' he had said. 'Congratulations!'

They had enjoyed that assignment – working together.

The woman let out a long moan. Despite the coolness in the air, perspiration beaded on her pale brow, and the man gently wiped her face with a cloth. To his credit, he was calm, thought Gilliad, but he could see the man was worried. A stable was no place for a woman to give birth. The man had tried to suggest that maybe the wife of the innkeeper could come and help the young woman, but she could not be spared.

'I am sorry,' the innkeeper had replied. 'She already has too much to do looking after the paying guests.' He put emphasis on the last two words. 'Perhaps I could send her out when she has finished cooking and washing the dishes,' he added, when he saw the man's face. But he never did.

And it was too late now anyway.

Latorius, who had taken to pacing backwards and forwards, now knelt down next to the woman. The man held her hand on the other side and in unison they both called out 'puuuush.'

Gilliad, who had been seated on the bale of hay, stood up and began to offer a running commentary for Latorius but, a moment later, it was over and the woman had given birth to her firstborn.

'Well done,' said Latorius, the proud midwife, as he stood up to inspect the infant.

The man could not speak. His eyes were filled with tears as he wrapped the tiny infant in cloths and handed him to the mother.

'I told you it wasn't twins.'

'Yes, you did,' agreed Gilliad, as they resumed their seats on the hay bale.

'Then we are both assigned to be the guardians of one child?'

'It appears to be so.'

'Have you heard of this happening before? Two guardians for one child, I mean,' wondered Latorius. 'It does seem somewhat out of the ordinary.'

'The Father commissioned us to this work. Gabriel sent us both here with the blessing of the Father.'

'Then I guess the reason will become clear. Until then, I will be guardian number one and you can be guardian number two.' Latorius looked sideways at Gilliad.

'I am not going to give you the satisfaction of a reaction,' said Gilliad, rolling his eyes.

'Just did.'

They sat on the bale of hay for some time, just watching the young mother's face. Gilliad always wished that, somehow, he could capture this moment: the very first moment when the new mother looked into the eyes of her newborn child.

The exhaustion and pain had disappeared now. Gilliad thought that it was almost as if the memory of the mother had been completely wiped of the moments that had led up to the birth, for in place of the pain, there was now wonder, joy, tenderness, and peace, and for hours after the birth, no matter how exhausted she was, she could not seem to take her eyes off that little bundle in her arms – that tiny miracle of life.

The infant was now wrapped tightly in soft white linen cloths, and as the mother held Him to her breast, she sang. It was a song to the Lord and Gilliad thought that he had never heard a more beautiful song – the song from the heart of the mother.

They watched as the man placed his hand upon the child's head and blessed Him.

The night had grown late. The streets around had quietened and the lights in the inn had long gone out. The man helped the tired mother to her feet and she carried her tiny newborn over to the manger and laid Him gently down on the bed of straw. The moon shone brightly through a high opening in the wall bathing the sleeping infant in a gentle bluish glow.

Finally, they could all rest.

The sound of a scuffle at the door interrupted the quietness of the night and outside in the yard a number of male voices spoke in urgent whispers. The baby stirred in His sleep, and the mother, who had been about to lie down again, returned to stroke the child's head and He quickly settled.

The man opened the door to investigate the disturbance and, at the same time, a number of bedraggled-looking figures spilled in through the opening, followed by the disgruntled innkeeper in a crumpled, heavily-stained, linen robe.

The shepherds. Gilliad recognised their voices even before they had reached the end of the short corridor between the animal stalls. The two boys came around the corner into the open area followed by their father who had them both firmly by the necks of their robes. The boys and their father were followed by the two older bearded gentlemen, who were slightly out of breath and arguing with the innkeeper in rapid bursts of Greek interspersed with passionate Hebrew utterances to each other.

The man motioned to the innkeeper his acceptance of the unexpected intruders and the innkeeper threw his hands up in the air, muttered something that Gilliad could not quite make out, and left them.

The innkeeper wasted no time in his retreat. The young man would just have to sort it out himself then. He had done his best. It would be another busy day tomorrow and he had had little sleep before the midnight hour. He would be up before dawn again, lighting the hearth and helping his wife prepare the morning meal for his guests before going down to the markets to buy food for the evening meal. His wife certainly could not spare the time to do this. He knew he would have to be early at the markets that morning, for all the other inns would need to stock up on supplies too, and it would be very bad for the inn's reputation if guests spread the word that the food at his inn was less than generous. Business was slow at the best of times. Except now, he thought. Yes, right now he found himself longing for peace and quiet. But ... there was little money to be made in peace and quiet.

The shepherds crowded around the tiny makeshift crib. They had not intended to burst in like that. In fact, they hadn't really worked out any sort of a plan once they had found the place. It just happened.

That was the problem with these young boys, the father of the shepherd boys thought. Always doing things before thinking. But he had been just the same at that age. He glanced at both of his boys, neither of whom had taken their eyes off the face of the infant since they had burst in through the door.

It was a while before any of them spoke. They just stood and looked.

The oldest of the shepherds eventually found his voice and began to relay their story to the man.

They had been out in the fields watching over their flocks. The older men had reached the end of their watch and had just woken the younger man and his sons. They had all gathered around the glowing coals of the fire. The father had stoked up the flames and thrown on a few more logs to heat some water. They sat for a while on their bed rolls, for the ground had cooled.

The father had poured out warm drinks to ease the chill in their hands and warm their bellies. They finished their drinks and walked over to check the sheep before the older men handed over to the father and his boys so they could, themselves, settle for the night.

The star they had observed earlier still shone brightly, even more brightly than before, or so it seemed, and it was now almost directly over their heads. It was easier to see the further away from the campfire they got, so they moved further back and stood with their backs to the fire, facing away from the glare.

As they stood there looking up into the sky, suddenly there was a brilliant flash of light, as if the sun had appeared in the night sky, and an angel of the Lord appeared to them.

'We were so scared,' the younger one offered.

'You were scared. I wasn't,' said the older boy.

'Were too.'

'Not.'

'Boys!' the father shot them a warning look.

The old shepherd continued. 'We were all a bit scared, truth be told. But the angel told us not to be afraid. "I bring you good news of great joy that will be for all the people," he had said. "Today in the town of David, a Saviour has been born to you: He is Christ the Lord. This will be a sign to you: You will find a baby wrapped in cloths and lying in a manger." We all looked at each other. I can assure you, we were not dreaming, nor had we had any strong drink. Not a drop. And the young lads here have never even touched the stuff.'

The boys nodded vigorously.

'Each of us saw the same things,' the old man continued. 'That is not all. While we were looking at each other, trying to understand the words the angel had spoken, the whole sky became filled with angels. And they began singing. It was beautiful.'

The old man began to weep and his brother took over.

'Yes, they certainly did sing. They sang beautifully,' he nodded to his brother, who was wiping his face with the dirty sash that hung around his waist. 'What were the words of the angel, boy?'

The older boy was pleased to be asked. He had memorised the words and had said them over and over in his mind, all the way in to town. 'Glory to God in the highest, and on earth peace to men on whom his favour rests,' he said, annunciating every word as if being tested by the rabbi in the synagogue.

'Well done, lad. Well done.'

'So you see, there was nothing for it but to come and find the babe,' said the older shepherd, finding his voice again.

They had left the sheep in the fields without a second thought, the father of the boys explained, feeling that it was perhaps his turn to pick up the story. After all, he had reasoned, if there are that many angels all around, surely for the remainder of the night, just this one night, the sheep would be safe.

By this late time, there were very few lights on in the town, and as they hurried through the streets, all was quiet. They had reached the centre of the town where most of the inns were and had stood for some time in the marketplace, uncertain. They looked around at all the signs. Closed. Full. No room. They wondered how they were ever going to find the child.

'The angel said the baby would be in a manger, didn't he?' the younger boy had said.

'Son, you are right!'

The inns that immediately surrounded the marketplace would not have mangers, for they did not have stables out the back. It was only the inns that lined the alleyways – those set further back from the marketplace – that were allowed to keep animals.

Nevertheless, that was a lot of inns.

'Well,' the father had said after they had stood for several moments, 'we have to begin somewhere.'

It didn't take them long to find the place, though. They began half-walking, half-running through the backyards of several small establishments, leaving a trail of bleating, mooing, and clucking animals in their wake.

Halfway down the second row of yards, they had been yelled at by an innkeeper's wife who had opened the backdoor to see what the commotion was about. 'Be off with you!' she had hollered, causing an even greater disturbance amongst the fowls nesting under the overhang of the inn's back roof.

When they had reached the end of that row of inns, they heard voices – a man's and a woman's – coming from the stable at the back.

'This one! It has to be this one,' the young boy had said in an all-too-loud voice.

The innkeeper had appeared at the back door. 'You there!' he yelled, and they stopped in their tracks. The light from the moon shone on his large belly and long white beard, and from the top of the steps he appeared a formidable figure. He had slipped out of bed when he had heard the yelling of the woman at the inn several doors down and had come out to investigate. He started down the steps towards them and the young boy ducked behind his father.

'What business do you have disturbing the whole of Bethlehem in the middle of the night?' He looked the shepherds up and down. 'This here's private property.'

'We have come to see the baby,' said the older shepherd.

'What baby? There is no baby in my inn.' But he knew that the woman, whom he had earlier shown into the stable, had given birth, for he had heard the cries of the baby.

'The baby who has been born in the stable.'

The boy's father had put his hand on the door of the stable and began to push it open, and the two boys, not needing a second invitation to put distance between themselves and the angry innkeeper, tumbled in through the doorway.

'Look, you can't just barge in there ...'

'Come and see,' said Latorius. The shepherds had gone now and peace had descended once more.

They crept quietly over to where the baby lay. They could have stomped and hollered and it would not have mattered, but where sleeping newborn babies were concerned, they usually behaved in an appropriate fashion.

The infant's face was perfect. There was a fine tuft of dark hair poking out from under the cloth that was wrapped snugly around His head. He had the beginnings of eyebrows: two tiny soft lines of downy hair, and in His sleep, He frowned.

As they watched, His lips parted. A tiny bubble was poised between them for a brief moment, and as He sighed, the tiny breath popped the bubble sending a minute spray of droplets into the air which landed on the fine hairs around His little mouth.

'He looks nothing like the father,' observed Latorius, looking from one to the other.

Of course Latorius would say something like that, thought Gilliad. He looked at the man, then back at the infant, then back at the man again. This time, he had to agree. He didn't like to suggest that there might have been some impropriety, but really, Latorius was right.

That surprised him. They had been with the little family long enough for him to have formed the opinion that the new mother was not that kind of young woman.

The baby's bottom lip quivered and began moving in and out. He yawned a big yawn, then opened His eyes for a moment, before screwing them up against the bright moonlight.

'He is beautiful. Perfect,' said Latorius. He said that about every baby he had had the privilege to guard. He could quite happily stand there and just look at them, every moment of every day.

As they bent over the manger and watched the face of the infant, He slowly opened His eyes again.

Gilliad gasped and looked at Latorius. 'The …'

But neither could speak, for once again, they found themselves looking into the eyes of eternity: the eyes of wisdom, of love. Once again, they found themselves looking deep into the eyes of the Son.

The Messiah – the Seed of the woman – the promise of long ago – had been born.

Also by J R Thomas:

Spirit Heart Soul – Origins & Destinies

Spirit Heart Soul - Origins & Destinies is the book that will tell you where you came from and where you are going. It will tell you where heaven is, where hell is, and how to get to one and avoid the other!

The fact is, we are spiritually disconnected from the source of life - our Creator. That is not how we were designed, and Adam and Eve were certainly not created in this state. The implications of still having this spiritual birth defect when you die are enormous. It means that you will be forever separated from the source of eternal life.

The good news that I share in the pages of Spirit Heart Soul - Origins & Destinies is that this condition - this birth defect - is reversible. This book will not only tell you how you came to have this spiritual birth defect, but it will also tell you the cure - a miracle cure that was costly, but it is free. It is a cure that will literally save your life!

This book contains the answers to the questions of life and death - answers found in the Bible. Why have I used the Bible to find answers? I believe that the Bible is the Word of God and therefore contains the truth. I believe that the answers to our origin and destiny as well as an understanding of the state of mankind due to sin can only be found in the Bible and that only the Bible contains the words of hope and life.

The accuracy and authority of the Bible as the Word of God has been proven through fulfilled prophecy, perfect coherence of the 66 books that make up the Holy Scriptures written by about 40 authors over about 1500 years (evidence of divine inspiration), archaeological evidence, the confirmation of historical facts in Scripture by other historical records, and by changed lives.

Embark on a journey with me, and as you travel through the pages of this book, you will uncover the truth about you ... God ... angels and demons ... heaven and hell. You will discover the way to forgiveness ... restoration ... eternal life.

You will discover the path of life that has no end.

276 pages

Available in softcover, hardcover, and eBook.

For further information visit:

www.jrthomas.com.au

www.ingramcontent.com/pod-product-compliance
Lightning Source LLC
Chambersburg PA
CBHW070110260626
47160CB00004B/1409